SCOURGE OF THE STEEL MASK

A G-8™ AIR-WAR THRILLER

BY ROBERT J. HOGAN

Cover Painting by Ken W. Kelly

DIMEDIA INC.
NEW YORK   CHICAGO

SCOURGE OF THE STEEL MASK

Originally published in
G-8 AND HIS BATTLE ACES Magazine, January 1937

Dimedia Edition, October 1985

Reprinted by arrangement with
Blazing Publications, Inc.,
successor-in-interest to
Popular Publications, Inc.

Dimedia, Inc.
P.O. Box 423
Oak Forest, Illinois 60452

ISBN 0-89300-240-2

Printed in the United States of America

CHAPTER ONE
Death Does Not Sleep

In the apartment end of the hangar at Le Bourget, daylight still streamed through the window and spread itself across the dining room table where G-8, the Master Spy, and his Battle Aces sat at supper. It was the evening the strange report came.

G-8 was slicing luscious slabs from the high roll of roast beef in front of him. He turned to Nippy Weston, the little terrier ace.

"You like it about medium, don't you, Nip?" he asked.

"Yes, thanks," Nippy nodded.

"And don't forget the way I like it," big Bull Martin broke in from the other side of the table. "For me it's got to be all red and juicy."

"Yes," G-8 nodded. "Seems to me I remember hearing something of the kind once or twice before. I don't know why anybody would ever bother to cook meat for you, Bull."

5

The big fellow grinned.

"They wouldn't need to—much," he admitted. He breathed deeply as he saw the sharp knife slice off a thick layer of rare roast beef for his portion. "Boy," he said, "that's what I call a meal! Rare, juicy roast beef, boiled potatoes with the beef juice all over them, boiled onions, rye bread." He eyed the portion of tomato salad in front of him. "Even that salad looks good," he said.

"Even that salad!" Nippy ventured. "Say, listen, you big ox, that salad of tomato and lettuce and Roquefort dressing is the best part of the meal."

Bull Martin laughed derisively.

"Oh, yeah?" he said. "Well, I suppose a little guy like you could live on what they serve at pink teas, but a man-sized human's got to have something to eat besides tomato and lettuce and a lot of stuff like that."

At that point, Battle, the manservant, cook, and master of make-up who stood at G-8's left elbow broke into the conversation apologetically.

"Oh, I say, the discussion of salad reminds me of a joke I heard a friend of mine—he happens to be bat man to General Compton—tell the other day. It's a deucedly good joke but a bit risque. I really hesitate to—er—"

With a grunt and a nod, Bull Martin took the overloaded plate that G-8 passed to him.

"Yeah," he said, "I'll bet this is going to be a honey when it comes. Go on, Nip, Battle wants to be coaxed."

The manservant's sober face turned hopefully to Nippy, but G-8 spoke first in a reproachful tone.

"I don't think you're quite fair to Battle, Bull," he said. "I'm sure he doesn't want to tell anything that would be offensive to us. After all, we have our code of what's right and wrong to live up to. I for one don't want Battle to tell anything that would warrant washing his mouth out with soap."

The Master Spy didn't need to turn and look at Battle to know that the English manservant's face had turned crimson.

"Oh, I say now," he protested. "Look here! It's not as bad as that. It's really quite an innocent joke, really nothing about—about anything you gentlemen had in mind, I'm sure. I was reminded of it by the salad, you know. I dare say, perhaps some of you have heard it already, although it was told to me as a very new joke."

Nippy forced himself to look grave.

"Oh well, Battle," he said. "It must be all right."

Battle smiled delightedly.

"Then you want me to tell it, sir?" he asked eagerly.

"By all means," Nippy assured him.

"Yeah," Bull growled. "Tell it and get it over with. Some day, Battle, you'll murder me. You'll catch me with a mouthful of food and I'll start laughing and choke to death."

"Oh, I say," Battle beamed, "that would be jolly—er—I mean to say, unique. But about this story, if you really want to hear it. It's about a salad—sort of a quizzer, you might say."

"A quizzer?" G-8 repeated.

"Oh, yes, quite. A riddle. You know, one of those things—when is a thingabob not a such and such? But it's not quite like that, sir. You see, sir, I ask you 'Why does a tomato blush?' And you, of course, helping me out, say 'I don't know. Why does a tomato blush?' Then I tell you the answer. Now do you understand? Shall we have a go at it, sir?"

8

G-8 nodded good-naturedly.

"I'm ready whenever you are," he said. "Shoot."

"All right, sir," Battle nodded. "Now I commence. I say, sir, why does a tomato blush?"

G-8 put on a great show of dignity and in a deep, bass voice answered, "I don't know, my good man. Why does a tomato blush?"

Battle beamed triumphantly.

"Because," he replied, "it sees the mayonnaise."

Nippy, Bull, and G-8 were seized by a simultaneous convulsion of laughter. It was then that Bull Martin almost choked as he had prophesied a moment before. There was much drinking of water and slapping of his back. When he was back to normal and could speak, he glared at the bewildered Battle.

"All right, you dumb cluck," he said, "I ought to murder you."

"Yes, sir," Battle nodded meekly. "I had a bit of a feeling that there was—er—something wrong with the joke. Do you mind doing it over again?"

"Maybe you should ask why is there a tomato?" Nippy cut in.

"Yeah," Bull growled. "What I've been wondering, is why is there a Battle?"

But G-8 wasn't joining in the banter now. He was sitting up straight in his chair, motionless, silent, listening. A split second later, Nippy and Bull caught the same sound that had come to his ears. From far away, a plane motor droned and grew louder rapidly.

"Somebody," G-8 said half to himself, "is heading here full out."

He rose to his feet as he uttered those words. Nippy and Bull were directly behind him as he reached the tarmac. From the northeast, a Nieuport marked with the French concentric circles came tearing in over the boundary of the field. It landed in two short bounds and swerved, taxiing rapidly toward the end hangar.

As the motor died, the pilot raised himself from the cockpit and began spouting French. He stopped suddenly as he reached the ground, panting for breath.

"Pardon, *messieurs*," he said. "I forgot you were Americans! *Mon Dieu*, I am so excited! I have been sent here from aerial headquarters at Toule to make a report. Perhaps you would be good enough to direct me to headquarters office. I must make my report directly to G-8. He is located here, *n'est-ce pas?"*

The Master Spy nodded.

"Yes," he said. "Come on. You won't have to go to headquarters. I am G-8."

"Mon Dieu!" the Frenchman exclaimed. "You are G-8?"

The Master Spy nodded again.

"Come in," he said. "Let's get at this thing immediately."

He led the way into the living room.

"You will pardon my excitement?" the Frenchman said. "I am located with the 11th flying corps at Epinar. That, *monsieur,* is far to the east,—well into the Vosges mountains."

G-8 nodded.

"Yes, I know," he said.

"There is practically no activity in our area," the Frenchman continued. "So I turned the nose of my plane this afternoon toward the Black Forest. There, *monsieur,* is where I came upon this strange happening.

"I had meant to go only a little way over the forest to get a good view of the great, dark area and see the shadows that the sun cast as it went down. Then I sighted a fair-sized captive balloon looming out of the tree tops. As I flew closer to investigate, I saw a basket hanging from it. There was a large man in it, dressed in a German uniform and holding an instrument of some kind. I decided it couldn't be a gun, because it had no opening at the end of the muzzle. In fact, it was plugged and larger there. Both the bag of the captive balloon and the basket bore a black cross.

"I aimed my guns and was about to fire when the man levelled his instrument at me and braced himself as though he were about to fire the weapon. At that instant, my engine stopped dead and I was forced to drop my nose sharply to keep my propeller from stalling."

"Was there any sound from this weapon that you mentioned?" G-8 asked.

The Frenchman shook his head.

"*Non,* none whatever."

"And what did you do?"

"There was a field below, *monsieur,*—one large enough for me to land in. But I saw that the cable from the balloon went down to the edge of this field and since I had a good altitude, I decided to try and get back near my own lines. I realized that this must be a trap in which to capture Allied planes. I kept my nose pointed down quite

12

sharply so that the wind would keep my propeller turning over although my engine was still dead. The German was still pointing his weapon at me. I knew that I couldn't possibly reach my own lines but I decided I'd rather crash in the Black Forest than be drawn down into that trap."

"But you didn't crash," Nippy cut in.

The French pilot shook his head.

"Non, monsieur," he admitted. "Just as I had given up hope, my engine began to splutter and it started running again. I flew directly to aerial headquarters to get gas and report what had happened. They sent me here."

As the Frenchman finished, G-8 walked to the wall and pressed the button in a signal for his plane to be brought on the lines. But he signalled for only his own Spad, a move that solicited frowns from both the Battle Aces.

"What's the idea?" Nippy demanded.

"I'm going out to see this thing for myself," G-8 told him. "There's no use of all three of us getting trapped. It sounds like the beginning of something pretty big and I want to stop it before it assumes any great proportions. If I'm not back by dawn, come after me."

He turned to the Frenchman, at the same time spreading out a map of the Black Forest area on the table.

"Now, lieutenant," he said, "would you mind showing me the exact spot where this balloon is located?"

"It will be a pleasure," the Frenchman agreed.

The grumble of G-8's Spad sounded out on the tarmac as the Master Spy studied directions and checked his watch with the setting sun.

"It's a long chance but I think I can just about make it before dark," he said. "Nippy, you call up Toule after I've started and tell them to have the gas truck on the line. I'll stop there to refuel."

Again he focused his attention on the map.

"I've been over that area," he told the Frenchman. "Do you remember seeing a large and very old castle sticking up out of the trees about two miles west of this point?"

The lieutenant nodded.

"*Oui, monsieur,*" he said. "That is La Rocque castle. There are many strange tales regarding it. I saw it this afternoon when I was near the balloon."

"One more thing," G-8 continued. "You said you believed that was a trap of some sort in which to catch Allied planes. What made you think that?"

"*Mon Dieu,* did I forget to tell you? There were already two captured Allied planes standing on the field. I saw the pilots trying to start their engines."

"You're sure they were Allied planes?"

"Positive, *monsieur.* One was a French Nieuport like mine, only from another squadron, and the other was a Salmson two-seater bearing American markings."

"You believe, then, that these planes were brought down by this strange weapon possessed by the German in the balloon basket?"

The Frenchman shrugged.

"To be sure, *monsieur,*" he said. "What else could it be?"

Bull Martin laid his great paw on G-8's shoulder.

"Listen, chief," he said. "Why don't you let me go on this job? I don't matter so much as you do and if I go down and get captured, you'll stand a lot better chance of helping me escape than I will of helping you."

G-8 smiled.

"Thanks for the offer, Bull," he said, "but I'm afraid I'll have to take this on myself. First hand information is always better than second, you know."

The Master Spy took his helmet and goggles from the mantel over the fireplace and strode out toward his ship.

CHAPTER TWO
Black Forest Magic

It was growing fairly dark as G-8 reached the southwest edge of the Black Forest. He could see the towering mountains shielded by the velvet foliage of spruce. The last rays of the setting sun touched the topmost spires, silhouetting them, in striking contrast to the deep gorge of black shadow. Beyond, the few remaining turrets of half-crumpled La Rocque castle loomed up menacingly.

The Master Spy leaned forward a little more intently and his eyes swept that ridge with a closer scrutiny. The map that he had inspected back at Le Bourget was well fixed in his mind. He was looking now at the exact spot a couple of miles this side of La Rocque castle where there should be a patch of a field large enough for an emergency landing, and a captive balloon hanging high above its mooring.

There was no balloon in the air now. The place where the field should be lay in dark shadow, so that at that distance and angle he couldn't see a field at all. Drawing nearer, he straightened in the cockpit, lifting his head so that he could look over the windshield and get a clearer view. He was certain that there was something moving in that pocket of gloom. He held a hand up to shield his eyes from the brilliant rays of the setting sun. That move permitted him to see more easily.

There was a huge object rising rapidly from the field. It was the big captive balloon edging into the air at the end of its cable with express-elevator speed. The balloon was at least a thousand feet up.

Through his powerful binoculars, G-8 made out a man in the basket. He was large and powerful—larger even than Bull Martin. He appeared to be wearing a Hun uniform, although at that distance, G-8 couldn't be quite sure. It was obvious that he was holding something in his hands just below the level of the basket's edge. That must be the strange weapon that the French lieutenant had spoken of.

All this G-8 saw from an altitude of little better than five thousand feet. He increased his altitude as he came nearer. He was still almost two miles away when he saw through the binoculars that the big fellow in the basket was raising the strange weapon. It seemed to be composed of a tube about an inch and a half in diameter and about three feet long. Wires trailed from the other end which was a little larger, not unlike the breach of a gun, although the muzzle had a small metal ball on the end as though someone had blown a bubble from it.

The Master Spy had planned carefully. He wasn't sure of this mysterious power, didn't know just what it would do to an airplane motor and he wasn't taking any more chances than necessary. He was above the balloon and to the southwest, so that he could dive down on it at an angle of about forty-five degrees. Thus, he wouldn't need his engine.

He closed the throttle and the Hisso died to idling. Then he cut his switch. His swift glide through the air kept the propeller turning but the motor was silent. He slipped his binoculars into their case at the side of the cockpit for he could see the figure in the basket very plainly now without them.

That strange weapon was being pointed up at him. All was still except for the screaming of the wind through his wings and brace wires. His main object in cutting his engine was that he might learn for certain whether this weapon made any sound at all. But nothing came from it—no sound, no light, no flame, no spark.

The balloon had stopped its ascent and was hanging motionless, swaying a little at the end of its cable in the light breeze. About two thousand feet separated them, but G-8 in his long gliding dive was shortening that distance rapidly. Fifteen hundred more and then he could get ready to fly with his Vickers.

The man in the balloon braced his big hulk against the basket and leaned farther over the edge, poking the weapon out into space as though that might give it more of the strange power it was supposed to possess.

The Master Spy was taking stock of his feelings and of what went on about him. If there was a strange force coming from that weapon, it seemed to have no effect on him.

But in the next instant, G-8 sensed something strange. His whole body seemed gripped rather gently by a force difficult to describe. It was as though there were something inside him trying gently to shrink him to a smaller size. Diving, he felt this power increase until it grew painful. He found it difficult to swallow. Desperately, frantically, he kicked the rudder and moved the stick to make sure he wasn't becoming paralyzed. He found that his muscles were working all right.

The space between his Spad's nose and the elephantine monster of the air was less than a thousand feet now. He pulled back the trips of his Vickers guns and dropped his head so that his eye lined over the sights. Two, three hundred feet more he raced. The bag seemed to be looming right off the muzzle of his Vickers. The strange force about him was terrific, yet he could still move all of his body at will. He jammed down his triggers and the Vickers guns clattered, hurling their incendiary bullets into the belly of the monster bag.

* * *

It seemed to G-8 that his shots were futile, but in the next instant, the mysterious force that had so painfully gripped him suddenly let go. He yanked the stick back as he saw that the portion of the balloon where his shots had entered was opening abruptly. From that huge gap, flames spewed up, licking toward his steeply-banking Spad.

His propeller was still turning. He adjusted the throttle and flipped on the switch and the engine barked out.

With that accomplished, G-8 turned to take stock of the situation. The entire balloon was a mass of flames. The man in the basket had thrown his weapon overboard and the Master Spy could see it hurtling to the ground.

Now the balloonist himself was climbing over the edge of the basket on the side where a canvas bag was tied. He poised there for an instant and plunged headfirst. As the balloon collapsed in a mass of flames, G-8 saw shroud cords shoot out and then the white chute was jerked from the bag and cracked open in full bloom.

The Master Spy circled lower as he witnessed a horrible sight. The Hun was swaying back and forth like a great pendulum at the end of his shroud cords. The expression on his face was ghastly with fear, for the burning remains of the balloon were hurtling down upon him. Desperately, he tried to slip the parachute to bring himself out from under that burning gas bag.

Then he struck. He had apparently maneuvered the chute so that the burning bag wouldn't fall on him, but in the last instant, his pendulum swing carried him under the flaming heat, leaving the parachute just at the edge.

In one swift glance, G-8 studied the field below and saw that none of the Hun's henchmen were coming to give him aid. There was a chance that he might be saved. He sent his Spad charging down to a quick side slip landing and was out of the cockpit before the plane had stopped rolling. The German's parachute was already flaming and the heat was so intense that G-8 could stand it only long enough to grasp a handful of shroud cords that stuck out from the great fire, hurl them over his shoulder, and start off on a dead run.

As soon as he had dragged the heavy body of the Hun out of the flames, he ran back to it. Even in that short interval, the German's clothing was burned almost completely off him. The flesh on the face seemed to be like putty, ready to fall off at the touch. A gaping mouth—all that was left of the features—opened a little. There was a quick intake of breath, a sobbing groan, and then the whole body went limp.

G-8 glanced about him again, but strangely enough, there were no Huns coming, even now. He ran to the place where the strange weapon had fallen, and picked up the battered and bent remains. As he turned, he saw the line of cable that had run from the balloon basket to a machine in a corner of the field. Beside the winch that controlled the raising and lowering of the great gas bag was another machine. There were glass tubes like queer-shaped electric light bulbs, a generator that appeared to be hooked up to the gas engine that operated the winch, and a mass of wires and coils which G-8 took down in his mind as completely as possible before he left.

His ship was still idling when he reached it. After stowing the battered weapon in the back of his cockpit, he climbed in and took the air, heading for Toule. There he refueled and took off again immediately for Le Bourget.

Gasoline flares were lighted at his home field to help him down to a landing. Nippy,

Bull, and Battle were waiting anxiously. G-8 told them what had happened as he rubbed the oil from his goggles.

"Oh, but I say!" Battle interposed, "You don't mean to tell me you went down and landed to save the life of the man you had tried to kill."

An amused smile crept over the Master Spy's face as he looked up at the English manservant.

"It does sound funny, doesn't it, Battle?" he admitted. "But then, on the other hand, I wouldn't want to see him burn to death if I thought there was a chance of saving him."

"By Jove, that's what I like about this air service," Battle enthused. "There's something sporting—something downright cricket about the whole business, you know."

Nippy and Bull had been examining the battered weapon that G-8 had brought back. At G-8's questions as to what they thought of it, they both shook their heads.

"Except for those wires coming through, there doesn't seem to be any sense to it," Bull said.

"I'm going to take it to a signal officer I know who's a wizard on wireless and electricity in general," G-8 said, getting up.

The long, low powerful roadster sped him rapidly to Paris where he found the signal officer working in his wireless laboratory adjacent to one of the wireless stations. G-8 introduced himself, although it was scarcely necessary.

The signal officer, Captain Billings, was a gaunt sort of man with somber eyes shielded by horn-rimmed glasses. A smile spread over his long, angular face as he rose to greet the Master Spy. He was immediately interested when his eyes fell upon the weapon and those same eyes widened when G-8 told him where he had gotten it and of the happenings that surrounded its discovery.

Captain Billings went to work at once dissembling the instrument, which proved to contain strange coils and wires, together with a small glass tube inside the metal ball at the end.

"I'm sorry it's so terribly battered," Billings said. "We might make something out of it if we got the right hook-up. I wish I could see the machine that operated it. You say there was a machine on the ground with a generator and glass tubes and coils?"

"Yes," the Master Spy nodded. "A couple of wires ran up the balloon cable and were attached to the rear end of this affair."

Captain Billings hummed softly to himself as he scrutinized, once more, various winding wires that he had carefully taken out of the instrument. He turned quite calmly to G-8.

"You know," he confessed, "I'd very much like to go and see that machine personally—if you could arrange it."

At first, G-8 was hesitant.

"It's located quite far back in Germany, Captain," he said. "It would be risky business to go and inspect it."

The captain smiled slowly again.

"You were there, were you not?" he asked.

The Master Spy was forced to smile.

"Yes, of course," he admitted. "But—well, after all, hops into Germany are my business. You're an electrical expert and a signal man. Do you know anything about flying?"

"I can handle a brace of machine guns, if that's what you mean," Billings told him. Again his eyes fell upon the dissembled instrument on the table before him. "Yes," he repeated, half to himself, "I would certainly like very much to see that machine." He turned to G-8 once more. "Could you take me tomorrow at dawn?" he asked.

"I'd be very glad to do that," G-8 said.

"But I want you to know what you're getting into."

"Do you think there will be any Huns waiting for us?" Captain Billings asked.

"There's no telling," G-8 admitted. "I hope we can decide that before we land. At any rate, if you wish to go, it's settled. I'll see you at the field at dawn."

The captain nodded and smiled.

"By all means," he said.

Captain Billings was there even before dawn. G-8 already had a D. H. two-seater out on the line, warming. Beside it was Spads "7" and "13". Bull and Nippy were going with them as convoy.

As they took the air, the two Spads climbed above, riding at a five hundred foot distance to keep a large "V" formation.

Captain Billings and G-8 droned toward the Front and the Black Forest beyond. The sun was peering over the horizon ahead of them when they landed at Toule to get more gas. That done, they flew on.

The entire sector appeared to be dead, and as far as they could tell, there were no other ships in the sky. G-8 sighted the turrets of La Rocque castle once more and then guided his ship toward the lone field where he had landed the evening before. No moving thing was in sight.

From the air, the Master Spy made out the charred, black earth where the flaming balloon had fallen. He circled the field once and prepared to land.

As he cut his motor, he heard Captain Billings call out from the rear cockpit, "The place seems to be deserted. I hope they'll give us a chance to inspect that machine."

"Yes," G-8 called back, but there was a note of uncertainty in his voice as he went down, searching the ground constantly. That burned body should be there just outside the circle of blackened ground but he couldn't seem to find it and that aroused his suspicions. He turned and yelled back, "Have your Lewis guns ready, Captain, in case any ground troops should attack us! If you get out of the ship keep your Colt ready for action!"

With a rumbling sound, G-8 brought the D. H. to a halt over by the charred circle. A few paces from the plane he stared down at a spot that was dark and moist with human blood.

"What's that mess?" Billings asked curiously.

"That," G-8 said, "is where the body of the dead German was lying." He pointed a few feet away. "See—there's the parachute harness with the shroud cords burned off."

*   *   *

Suddenly, the Master Spy dropped to his hands and knees and began examining the ground about the ugly, dark pool.

"That's funny," he said. "The earth is fairly soft here but I can't find the foot prints of whoever carried the body away."

"Is that important?" Billings asked a little impatiently. "I'd like to spend all the time I could looking over that weird machine you described to me."

G-8 got up.

"O. K.," he said. "It's over here at the edge of the woods."

He said nothing more about the vanished body but led the way around the patch of burned grass to the edge of the timber. There he stopped suddenly.

"There is no use going any farther. Look!" He pointed ahead at a small space, perhaps four feet wide and ten feet long, where the brush had been been either trampled down or cut away. "That, Captain Billings," G-8 said "is where the machine I described to you was standing. As you can see, it's gone."

"You mean, then, that I won't get a chance to look it over?"

"I'm sorry," G-8 said, "but that's the way it looks."

"But who could have—" Billings began.

"I don't know," G-8 cut in. "That's what I'd like to find out. There's no trace of anyone coming to carry them away."

Nippy and Bull were droning in a wide circle a few hundred feet above the field while G-8 and Captain Billings made their search. Suddenly, the air below was split wide open with a roar that belched from the short stacks of Spads "7" and "13." Down over the field the two Battle Aces thundered and the short staccato notes of Vickers guns were heard.

At the first sound of the diving planes, G-8 had turned and run into the clearing at the corner of the field. Nippy was very low in a long dive and Bull was riding his tail. They were yelling like maniacs, cutting their motors so that they could be heard:

"Shove off! Huns coming!"

Captain Billings blinked behind his thick glasses and G-8 grabbed him by the arm.

"Come on!" he barked. "Get into that cockpit! We're hopping off right now!"

As he spoke, he stared up in search of the enemy planes. He saw them screaming out of the east—a six-plane flight of

Fokkers. In his mind, the Master Spy was trying to figure out his chances of getting into the air and away before they came. Somehow, he didn't have too much confidence in the captain's air fighting ability.

Captain Billings had gotten his long legs in the rear cockpit and was squatting down on the seat. Meantime, G-8 was in the pilot's cockpit, batting the gun open. The Liberty thundered out and wings began to lift.

As they topped the trees Spandau guns began chattering, but G-8 knew that they were aimed at Nippy and Bull who had climbed up to intercept the approaching planes.

The mixed chatter of Spandau guns and Vickers grew nerve-shattering. At first, G-8 made a dash for it, but in spite of Nippy and Bull's efforts, half the Fokkers charged down and the D. H. was caught in volleys of cross-fire. Spandau lead pounded through the covering of the plane. The Lewis guns were silent.

G-8 yelled to the captain, "Drive them off your tail! What do you think you're back there for?"

Captain Billings was struggling with the guns, trying to swing them on their Scarf mounting, but somehow he couldn't make out the handles that would permit them to whirl easily.

Frantically, G-8 tried to show him how to put them into operation. He saw a burst of lead from one Fokker slam directly into the back cockpit, and Captain Billings went down. The Master Spy dropped the nose of the D. H. and pulled up again, then sawed the rudder over to the right. As she lumbered up and came over, his sights were trained on a Fokker with a green body and black wings. His triggers went down and his nose guns began chattering. There was a puff of flame and the wings and tail of that Fokker protruded from a gigantic bonfire that hurtled earthward.

The Master Spy swung down and levelled off. As he made a desperate attempt to start home, dodging over the tree tops, he realized that his ship had suddenly become nose-heavy. He spun around and stared back, but even before his eyes fell upon the empty cockpit, he saw the body of Captain Billings, limp arms and legs flopping wildly, falling through space.

Fokkers droned on behind him, their slugs pounding again and again into the D. H.'s covering. Nippy and Bull were making it very difficult even for that number of Fokkers. Minutes passed and the race for the lines continued. G-8 couldn't put up much of a fight in that lumbering D. H. with the rear cockpit empty.

As they crossed the Front, the Fokkers gave up the chase and turned back. G-8 and his Battle Aces landed to refuel.

"Hey, didn't you tell your observer to strap himself in?" Nippy demanded.

"I did," G-8 answered. "Remember, I told him about it when we left Le Bourget and again when we left Toule on the way up. I had a job arguing him into it the second time. It didn't matter anyway. I've got a pretty good hunch he was dead before he dropped out. With the Spandau slugs that went into him before I pulled up and over, he didn't have a chance. Too bad; we've lost a valuable man. But what concerns me most is the disappearance of the machine and the German that was burned."

"Maybe he got up after you left and took his machine and walked off," Bull suggested.

G-8 shook his head.

"You wouldn't have thought so," he said, "if you'd seen him when I left. As a matter of fact, he died while I was there beside him."

CHAPTER THREE
Herr Stahlmaske

A cry rang out, shattering the dawn still-
ness of the town of Waldheim in the south-
western foothills of the Black Forest. Before
the small hospital stood a young lad, his
face turned up toward the windows above
the entrance. He shouted:

"*Herr Oberdoktor! Herr Oberdoktor!*
Come quickly. I have in my cart—" as he
called, the window was thrown open, and
a man with glasses and close-cropped beard
cut in:

"*Was ist?* What are you yelling about?"

The eyes of the hospital head traveled
beyond the boy to his dog-drawn, two-
wheeled cart. There were three shining
milk cans, shifted to one side of the cart.
The rest of the small vehicle was crowded
to overflowing with the remains of a human body so ghastly to look at that the
Herr Doktor, before thinking, burst out
with:

"*Lieber Gott,* why do you bring a burned corpse to the hospital?"

The lad's face was white and his voice was unsteady but he was in earnest.

"*Bitte, Herr Oberdoktor,*" he said. "He is not dead. He—"

The lad got no further, for the huge, limp form in the cart suddenly grunted and moved. The sound that came from the lipless mouth caused the lad to shrink in horror.

Locks grated from the inside of the hospital door and it burst open before the *Herr Oberdoktor.* Assistants followed with a stretcher.

Another groan and gurgle came from the burned man while he was being picked out of the cart and placed on the stretcher. The *Herr Oberdoktor* saw the litter start for the hospital entrance and turned to the lad.

"Now tell me, *meine Junge,* who is he and where did he come from *und* who are you?"

The boy tried to control his tremblings.

"I am Hans Shilder, *Herr Doktor,* but I do not know who this poor burned one is. I was coming from my father's little farm in the mountains beyond La Rocque Castle. Always, my dog Troll and I have to start

35

with the milk before daylight. You know the stories they tell about La Rocque Castle, *Herr Oberdoktor?*"

"Yes, yes, of course. Hurry. I must get back. Tell me where you found him and—"

"I am coming to that, *Herr Oberdoktor,*" the boy cut in breathlessly. "I am always afraid going past the cliff of rock on which stands the ghost castle. This morning I heard someone move beside the road and next I heard a most awful sound—like he made just now. *Mein* dog, Troll, was sniffing and turning out of the road to the right. There I found him, *Herr Oberdoktor.* I wanted to run, but my legs would not carry me away."

The *Herr Oberdoktor* frowned.

"Did you hear him mention any name?"

"*Nein, mein Herr.* I could understand very little that he said. He made me understand that he wanted to be brought to the hospital.

"You did well," the *Herr Oberdoktor* smiled. "You are a brave lad."

He patted the boy's shoulder, then he hurried into the hospital.

The *Oberdoktor's* assistant met him inside with a shake of his head. Walking rapidly down the corridor beside the *Ober doktor,* the assistant spoke with marked excitement.

"There is no use, *Herr Oberdoktor.* He cannot—he must not live. He would be horrible to look at—too horrible to force upon normal humans. Already the flesh is falling from his face."

They reached the door of the operating room. *Herr Oberdoktor* gave a short nod and passed inside.

"We shall see," he said.

There, over the operating table, the *Herr Oberdoktor* and his assistant worked long hours. At the end, the *Oberdoktor* shook his head.

"Only by a similar miracle such as that which kept him alive thus far, can he go on living."

But the great burned corpse did live.

Weeks later he rose from the hospital bed and looked at himself in the mirror. A cry of horror escaped the hole in his mouth as he stared at the ghastly face and head that were his.

"*Lieber Gott!* Something must be done. You must build a new face."

The *Herr Oberdoktor* was standing beside him. "I am sorry," he said. "We have done all possible. The fire did its work too well. Flesh and skin will not adhere—to what is left. It is, of course, a miracle that you live."

"Live?" the big Hun grunted. "Live? You expect me to live—like this?" A hollow, cackling laugh rang out through the hospital with a strange, echoing sound as though it came from within a great barrel. "*Dass ist gut!* I should go on living with no face at all—with nothing but a skull that has holes in the front of it—and no name!"

"Perhaps your name will come back to you," the *Herr Oberdoktor* ventured.

"Nein," croaked the Hun. "It shall never come back to me. I go on from here with the past, except for one thing, blotted out. I shall have a steel mask made, and I shall be known—and feared—as *Herr Stahl maske. Und* you—"

He swept the hospital room and its occupants, curious doctors, with eyes that blazed red from the skull-face. Scant muscle tissues, that served to hold the jaw on and made the face still more ghastly, tightened. A yell burst from the teeth-rimmed mouth.

"I hate you all. I hate every man and woman who is normal!"

* * *

A newcomer entered the room, bearing a package wrapped in paper. The *Oberdoktor* advanced to meet him, holding out his hands. When he had taken the package, he turned to *Herr Stahlmaske* and tendered it to him with a bow.

"I have anticipated your needs, *Herr Stahlmaske*," he announced. "I had this steel mask prepared against the time when you would leave the hospital. May I present it to you with our deepest sympathy?"

Stahlmaske turned his huge bulk, and picked the mask from its wrappings. It was glistening and ugly-looking. It rose on the sides like a wide stovepipe, while at the top it came together in a dull point. It was made of heavy steel with openings in front and at the sides for sight, hearing, breathing and speech.

Slowly, like one condemning himself to a chained eternity, *Stahlmaske* turned to the glass, raised the mask helmet and slipped it over his head. For a moment he stood, his big body trembling with hatred and emotion, then he turned and faced the doctors once more.

"There," he said. "Perhaps I appear much less offensive?"

His eyes glowed crimson through the wide slits at the top of the helmet and fell upon the *Oberdoktor*. "You will tell me now where I am to find the *Herr Leutnant* who recognized the *Amerikaner* who is to blame for my being like this?"

"*Bitte,* he went back to his duties," the *Herr Oberdoktor* apologized, "after he left this note. The name is written here."

He handed *Stahlmaske* a slip of paper. A few words were scrawled across the sheet. He read:

> I have every reason to believe that the *Amerikaner* who shot you down was the *verdammt* one, G-8.

"*Gut,*" *Stahlmaske* croaked. "I go now, *Herr Oberdoktor.*"

For days *Stahlmaske* roved from city to city, recruiting the ugliest of humans as his assistants. But, of all that motley crew he assembled in old La Rocque Castle, none was so horrible-looking as *Stahlmaske* himself.

On the night that he established his headquarters there, he spoke to them in that hollow, inhuman voice of his.

"I have picked you to work with me as my assistants. Other humans look upon us as brutes.

"You wonder why I have brought you

here and what you are to do. Know this, that when I was placed in this condition, I was experimenting with a wireless beam. When we have perfected the *Loscher* ma chine, then we begin, each with an instrument."

The blazing eyes of *Stahlmaske* swept the ugly brutes assembled before him.

"But there is another beam invention I must have. Which of you know the city of Freiburg best? Step forward."

Two advanced. One was tall and agile, with broad but stooped shoulders and one side of his face almost completely gone. The other was squat and built like a bull, with a head that seemed a little larger than a pea atop the extremely thick neck. The face that he had was a mass of scars and sores.

"Do you know where *Herr Doktor* Frie linger lives in Freiburg?" *Herr Stahlmaske* asked.

The heads of the two bobbed in agreement.

"Tonight, then," *Stahlmaske* finished, "you and I make a visit to the *Herr Doktor*. He is one of the *Vaterland's* most learned electrical wizards. Before, I would not dare steal him and his machine, but now—we

41

bring him back, together with the newest development in wireless beam. Come."

Under cover of darkness, they advanced on Freiburg. Reaching the house where the taller of the two brutes said that *Herr Doktor* Frielinger lived, *Stahlmaske* knocked softly. They heard the gentle steps of a woman, then *Frau* Frielinger opened the door and peered into the night.

Her mouth opened to emit a scream, but no sound came. *Stahlmaske* leaped for her, and clapped one huge paw over her face.

"Now," he boomed. "Where is *Herr Dok tor* Frielinger?"

The door was closed and all three brute men were inside. *Stahlmaske* released his hold just enough so that she could speak.

"I will not tell you where he is," *Frau* Frielinger choked.

She was struggling wildly, pitifully. From the back room of the house where a light glowed; a boy's voice called:

"Who is it, *mutter?*"

The next second he came running into the front hall. He stopped at the sight of the horrible figures, his eyes widened. The two others lunged for him, but the boy was quicker and leaped away, darting into the back room.

Stahlmaske barked a command: "Stop him!"

He pushed the mother away, holding her with his huge, scarred left hand, and doubling his right, struck her full in the face, felling her where she stood.

The two men held the struggling boy when he reached the sitting room. There on the table, beneath the lamp, were his studies that he had been doing in the peace of their home.

A brute laugh leaped from the mask as the huge one snatched the boy to him. For an instant, the red eyes burned at the face of the lad, then came that hollow laugh again.

"You are good to look upon, *meine Junge*," he croaked. "You will grow up to be an attractive man—such as I was—if your face is left to grow. Let us see what we can do to make you look like us."

Stahlmaske dug his finger nails deep into the flesh of the face, ripping parts off. The boy screamed, *Stahlmaske* laughed and ripped through again. Even the two brutes, who stood aside watching, shuddered at the sight.

The boy sank to the floor, shrieking with pain, and *Stahlmaske* kicked him in the temple. There was no more sound from him.

"Was ist?"

A mild voice sounded from a side door of the room as *Stahlmaske* turned from his awful work. A meek little man with nose glasses and a firm, determined chin looked in, then gasped in horror.

His face blanched as he stared at the three figures. He leaped across the room as he caught sight of his son lying on the floor with mangled head pillowed in a pool of his own blood.

The great arm of *Stahlmaske* lashed out and beat him back, and by the time the man had recovered his balance, the two brutes were holding his struggling form.

"You are *Herr Doktor* Frielinger?" *Stahl maske* demanded.

Fighting vainly, the prisoner cried out:

"Of course I am *Herr Doktor* Frielinger. What has that to do with my son? What have you done to him? Where is *meine frau*? Why are you here?"

"Those questions shall be answered later, *Herr Doktor*," *Stahlmaske* said with a low bow. "*Aber,* for now—"

The great right fist smashed out full in the *Herr Doktor's* face. His glasses shattered and his head snapped back and his body went limp.

"Be ready to move quickly," *Stahlmaske* ordered. "I go to the laboratory."

He returned several minutes later with several strange-looking machines and coils. The brute assistants carried the unconscious *Herr Doktor* Frielinger and the loot from his laboratory into the waiting car.

Stahlmaske had done his work on *Herr Doktor* well. The electrical wizard did not regain consciousness until long after he was brought to La Rocque Castle, high in the Black Forest.

As he awoke, he cried out with pain.

"My eyes!" he choked. "They burn like fire! What has happened? Turn on the lights. Where am I?"

The barrel voice of *Stahlmaske* came back:

"You need no light, *Herr Doktor*," he chuckled. "You are in the cell in the east tower. The rays of the sun are already falling across you, but you cannot see them. You are blind!"

"Blind!" The word that *Herr Doktor* Frielinger repeated came in a whisper. He nodded slowly, resignedly. "*Jawohl* I remember. A fist was coming at me very fast. My glasses shattered and the pieces are in *mein* eyes. That is what burns so. *Lieber Gott!"*

Stahlmaske laughed again and this time some of the brutes about him joined in the demoniac chuckled.

"Bitte," Herr Doktor Frielinger said feebly, "would it be possible to give me hypodermics so that the pain of the ground glass will be lessened?'"

"Hypodermics?" croaked *Stahlmaske.* "That is *gut.* Do you know why you have been brought here? So that you may describe to us the full secret of this beam machine. As soon as you have done that, hypodermics will be given and you may rest."

"The secret of *mein* extinguishing beam?" Frielinger's voice shook with emotion. *"Ach, Gott!* So that is it!"

"You have tortured *mein* son. You may torture or kill me, but I shall never let the secret of my extinguishing beam be known."

"No?" *Stahlmaske* barked. "We shall see. Men, first we string him to the ceiling by his thumbs. His feet will be fastened to that rack that I have brought from the dungeon. We begin the stretch!"

Stahlmaske superintended the preparations for torture. When *Herr Doktor* Frielinger was strung up, he was left there, groaning, half-conscious.

"Now," *Stahlmaske* said, "we go to make a test of this apparatus."

Below, in the crumbled expanse of what had once been the castle banquet hall, *Stahlmaske* eyed his men.

"Can any of you speak English at all?"

Several stepped forward.

"I shall pick the—" he broke off to laugh hideously—"best looking of you." He designated four of the group. "You are to go to Le Bourget field near Paris and bring back G-8. By the time you return, I will have the machine working properly. If this beam performs as I expect, it shall eat the *verdammt* one away, one limb at a time."

"*Aber*," one of the chosen argued. "That is enemy territory and we cannot speak well enough to pass for *Amerikaneren* or *Englishers*. We will be—"

Stahlmaske leaped for him, striking him such a blow with his open right palm that it knocked the ugly brute to the floor.

"I give the orders here," *Stahlmaske* shouted. "*Und* I make the plans. We have no arguments. *Verstehen sie?*"

Horrible heads nodded in the affirmative. There was a sudden tinge of fear that had not been there before. *Stahlmaske* was king.

"*Und* now," *Stahlmaske* went on. "*Eine minute*. I write a warning to the *verdammt* one."

From the desk he took paper and ink and began scribbling. When he had finished a short note, he folded it, placed it in an envelope and sealed it. On the front he wrote:

PERSONAL TO G-8

"Here," he barked, turning to the nearest of his tense, respectful brutes. "See that that is flown to Le Bourget at once and dropped outside the apartment door at the end hangar."

It was the gaunt, stoop-shouldered one with the half face who left.

Stahlmaske turned to those chosen for G-8's abduction.

"*Und* now," he thundered, "I give you the details for the capture."

CHAPTER FOUR
The Devil's Messenger

In the apartment of the end hangar at Le Bourget, Battle was calling G-8 and his Battle Aces into the dining room.

"If you ask me," Bull ventured as he took his seat and dove into the ham and eggs and fried potatoes, "this man's war will be over pretty quick."

"Nobody asked you, you big ox," Nippy jibed.

G-8 smiled. "Let him go on, Nippy," he urged. "Maybe Bull's decided, since everything has been quiet for so long, that he's going in for fortune-telling."

"Nuts!" was Bull's retort. "Lay off, will you? I was just thinking out loud."

"You ought to know," Nippy grinned, "that when you think, its time to declare a holiday. That's for ordinary thinking, but when you think out loud—Jumping Jupiter—that *is* something."

"Alright, you birds," Bull grumbled over

an ample slice of ham. He pointed his fork menacingly at Nippy. "But you see what I tell you. Heine's giving up. We haven't had a good bunch of trouble in over a month. I never saw things so quiet since Aunt Aggie—she was the talker of our family—got laryngitis and lost her voice."

"Beggin' your pardon, sir, but could I get you something more?"

Bull nodded and pushed his plate toward the manservant.

"Fill her up again, will you, Battle?" he requested. "You seem to be the only one around here who thinks I'm worth anything."

"Yes, sir, quite," Battle bowed, taking the plate. "And may I say, sir, that you are the most appreciative glutton I've ever cooked for?"

Bull drew back his arm in a playful gesture and Battle ducked.

"Go on," the big fellow boomed. "Get out and fill up that plate or I'll wrap you around the stove pipe."

"And while you're out there," Nippy called, "look in the ice box and see if you can figure out why the tomato is blushing."

"Seriously," Bull said, turning to G-8, "have you got any dope that tells you the

Heines aren't just about ready to lay down and call it a finished war?"

G-8 opened his mouth to speak, but instead he closed it again and rose slowly, noiselessly, from his chair. The sound of a screaming engine came to all. In another second, G-8, Nippy, and Bull, were running for the door that opened onto the field.

Out of the northeast, a screaming thing with wings grew larger. As it passed the trees at the end of the field, the nose dropped and it came roaring down the tarmac, straight for the end hangar and G-8 and his Battle Aces. Over their heads a message streamer ribboned out and fell lightly to earth while the Fokker flew on.

G-8 tore the note from the sack at the end of the streamers. Nippy and Bull stared at it over G-8's shoulder and together they read:

You thought you saw me burn to death more than a month ago, but although I tasted death I did not die.

Mein Loscher is nearly perfected. I will test it upon you.

Herr Stahlmaske

"Herr Stahlmaske," Bull snorted. "I never heard of him."

"I don't get it," Nippy chirped at the same time. "What does he mean by *'Loscher'* and who—"

G-8 had spun around and was yelling to the hangar mechanics to start their engines.

"There's no time, now, to explain," he barked over his shoulder as he ran to give them a hand. "You birds know German. Figure it out for yourselves. "Come on!"

Three Spads were roaring on the line. G-8 climbed into his cockpit and yelled orders to Nippy and Bull.

"Got to follow that Fokker and find out where he lands. That will probably be the seat of the trouble."

For almost two solid hours they chased the Fokker. Strangely, the enemy ship did not swing over to its own side of the lines, but headed in a straight course for the farthest eastern front.

G-8 began reconstructing that flight. His own gasoline was getting low. Fokkers didn't have any wider cruising radius than Spads; therefore, it would have been impossible for this Fokker to come from that eastern salient and return without stopping along the route for fuel.

They had swept over Nancy, and far ahead the Vosges mountains loomed. That meant that the Black Forest would be on the other side.

Already G-8 was satisfied as to the general location of the note sender who called himself *Herr Stahlmaske*.

G-8 turned then and signalled Nippy and Bull to turn back. They thundered high over the Vosges mountains in the twilight and dropped down at Nancy for refueling.

Questions flew at him fast when the three were out of their cockpits.

"Hey," Nippy chirped. "What did you mean by that crack about us knowing our German?"

"Yeah, and what's this note got to do with the guy that burned to death more than a month ago?" Bull wanted to know.

"Come on," G-8 encouraged. "I want to telephone and on the way I'll tell you what I can. I meant, Nippy, that you two should know what was meant by *'Stahlmaske'* and *'Loscher'*."

"Sure," Nippy nodded. "*'Stahlmaske'* means 'steel mask.' But what's that got to do with—"

"Listen, squirt," Bull cried triumphantly, "for once I can figure something out ahead of you. Sure, *'Stahlmaske'* means 'steel mask,' and I just got the hookup. This guy that G-8 thought was burned to death, lived. His face was so badly burned that he goes around wearing a steel mask and calling himself that. How's that G-8?"

"Swell," the Master Spy said. "Nice figuring, Bull."

"Jumping Jupiter!" Nippy cut in. "Somebody must have told you. You sure didn't figure that out by yourself."

"Nuts to you," Bull growled. A pause and then the big fellow said gravely. "There is one thing I can't remember or figure out, though. I don't recognize that German word, 'Loscher'."

"Loscher," G-8 explained, "means 'extinguisher'. A blotter-outer, an exterminator."

"Sure," Nippy cut in. "Anybody would know that."

Bull was paying no attention to the terrier ace than a great Dane would to a yipping Pomeranian.

"But," the big fellow persisted, "what would that have to do with a guy who got burned and is wearing a steel mask?"

"Remember," G-8 reminded him, "that this big German I shot down was experimenting with some kind of an electrical machine that would stop plane engines. He's probably referring to it as the machine that extinguishes running motors, like a fire extinguisher would put out a fire."

"Yeah?" Nippy chirped. "Well, try and figure this one out, then! He says his exterminating machine is about finished and he's going to try it out on you. Think he means he's just going to stop your machine with it?"

"You're right," Bull agreed. "G-8, he's got something more than a machine that will stop airplane engines. Suppose he has some kind of a beam or someting that will exterminate a human being or an airplane."

"Then," G-8 said, "we'll have to exterminate it."

They had reached headquarters, where the commander greeted them and tendered the use of his office. G-8 began a swift check by phone of the Fokker's whereabouts before it had reached Le Bourget. Minutes dragged into a half hour but finally he turned from the phone, satisfied.

"It's quite evident," he told the others, "that the Fokker bringing the note left from one field and flew back to another. My check-up shows that it came from somewhere opposite Verdun and flew back to the region of Freiburg in the Black Forest, a hundred and fifty miles away."

"That means," Bull ventured, "that this

bird who calls himself *Stahlmaske* has his headquarters somewhere near Frieburg."

"I think so," G-8 agreed. "Although I can't be sure."

Meantime, their engines had been running on the line after their refueling, awaiting their departure. Other ships were being tested on the great Nancy airdrome. The rumble had been almost constant since their arrival in Headquarters. Now, suddenly, during a lull in the conversation, all else became suddenly still.

The field commander turned, frowning perplexedly.

"What caused that?" he demanded. "Those engines have been running on test. They all stopped at once!"

G-8 was listening tensely. He was on his feet, charging for the door. The others followed.

Several planes were standing about the apron with mechanics staring at them in the dim light of dusk.

"What happened?" the booming voice of the C.O. demanded.

"We don't know, sir," a corporal saluted. "We were testing our ships, Tim and me, and all at once, they both went off."

"Come on to the motor blocks," G-8 advised.

Back of the repair hangar were motor blocks, built of heavy timbers, and there were engine beds where the Libertys and the Hissos and others could be bolted down and run on test to make sure mechanical repairs had been done well. But the motor test blocks were silent, and there again stood mechanics scratching their heads and asking vague questions of each other.

G-8 whirled to face the field commander.

"This," he said, "is serious, sir. Will you call aerial headquarters and advise that nothing be mentioned of this? The lips of every mechanic must be sealed tightly. We can't have the news of this getting to the enemy side of the lines. Do you understand, sir?"

"Exactly," the C.O. agreed. "I'll attend to it at once."

He left on a trot for headquarters office. G-8 faced Nippy and Bull.

"Feel anything funny?" he asked in a low voice. "Stand still and see."

There was a tense silence. Bull was first to speak.

"I do," he hissed in an awed whisper. "I feel as though somebody was trying to make me smaller."

"Yes," G-8 nodded. "That's pretty close. It's going away now."

Another tense pause and then:

"It's gone," Nippy breathed. "Let's see if our engines will start."

Hissos barked. Mechanics wound up other engines and they were roaring out over the field once more. G-8 and Nippy and Bull were climbing into their cockpits. The C.O. came trotting back from headquarters.

"I've given the aerial commander your advice. He will put through an order at once," he yelled above the idling motor.

"Good," G-8 called back. "We're going back to Le Bourget. If anything more turns up, call me there."

Then Hissos were gunned and the three Spads swept off the ground and headed for home.

CHAPTER FIVE
Battle's Sacrifice

Hours before, back at Le Bourget, Battle had watched the three Spads chew their way into the evening skies. He stood in the doorway, muttering to himself:

"There must be something beastly important about. I haven't seen the master go tearing away like that in weeks. There was a note dropped by a German plane. I wonder what it could have said."

With a face unusually blank, Battle turned inside when the drone of the three Hissos had died away. He cleared up the mess from the evening meal and was about to go to his room when he heard the jangling of the telephone bell on the living room wall.

Picking up the receiver, Battle called into the mouthpiece:

"Righto, who is there?"

A strange voice came back to him.

"*Iss* G-8 dere?"

Battle opened his mouth to speak, but left it that way without pushing any words out. His usually slow brain was going round and round, gradually working out a problem. He put his lips to the mouthpiece again and asked, to make sure:

"I beg pardon—I'm afraid I didn't get it, sir."

The voice at the other end repeated:

"*Iss* G-8 dere?"

That made Battle certain. The voice was distinctly German in accent, and Germans were enemies. He didn't stop to figure how one would be on his side of the lines talking to him on a telephone. He only thought of G-8 and of his trust in him. Battle was thinking faster than he had ever thought in his whole life.

"Yes, sir," he lied. "The master is right here. I'll call him, sir, in a moment. Remain there and—er—hold everything."

Battle covered his tracks so well that he even laid down the receiver so that it would make a sound over the wire. He went into the kitchen and began talking in normal voice.

" 'Hello. Yes. Quite so.' No, confound it. I can't seem to get away from the blasted way of saying it. But I must! I must take the place of G-8 until he returns. I have a feeling that he is in great danger and that this person on the phone is coming to do him harm. I must carry on.

"Where was I? Oh, yes, of course. "Hello! Yes. What do you want? Right to'—blast it, I mean, 'I see'."

Finished, but only half-satisfied, Battle went back to the phone and picked up the receiver gingerly. He lowered his voice.

"Hello!"

"*Iss* dat you, G-8?" asked the voice at the other end.

"Yes," answered Battle.

"I will come over right away," the voice gutturaled. "I haff just returned from de odder side and I bring information for you. You will wait for me?"

"Righto," Battle blurted and then: "I mean, yes, of course—or—"

He heard the receiver click at the other end of the line and hung his own on its hook. He walked to the center of the room and stared about more blankly than ever, mumbling and talking to himself.

"I must make up like the master. Yes, of course. They must mistake me for him and then I shall do my best to carry on until G-8 comes back to surprise them. But he must not walk into any trap."

He glanced at the clock over the mantel.

*　*　*

"It will be several hours before he comes back. Confound it! I wish I knew how long it will be before this fellow who sounds like a German will be coming here."

Battle was hopping about like a beheaded chicken.

"Dash it, what shall I do first?"

He solved that by getting out the old make-up box. With it before him, he sat down in front of the great mirror and, with deft touches, began transforming his face so that it grew more and more like that of the Master Spy.

When he had finished, he hastily put on one of G-8's uniforms. Battle groaned as he looked himself over in the big mirror for the final time.

"Blast it!" he breathed. "I'd make out well enough as a scare crow, but as the Master Spy—" He shrugged his slim shoulders that came inches from filling out the uniform coat. "I'll have to have a fling at it, however. I never was meant to impersonate anyone else but myself."

Battle paced anxiously from the living room into the kitchen and back again. He was mumbling to himself again. He made four round trips before he could make up his mind, then he turned on the oven in the kitchen so that it would go full blast, took a pot of beans that he had prepared to bake and placed them in the heating oven.

"Perhaps that will do," he ventured. "I was going to bake the beans this evening, anyway. But I fancy the way I have the heat turned that they'll be burning about the time the master returns. Meanwhile, who knows what will happen?"

Everything was ready. Battle fingered the automatic in the holster at his side from time to time. He sat down in a chair before the door and took out the big Colt, handling it as gingerly as though it were a small, poisonous beast.

"Ugh!" he shuddered. "When I think what this might do to one's insides, I—er—"

He stuffed it quickly back in the holster and leaped up. Darting from one window to another, he pulled down window shades with a loud, fluttering sound of haste. He stood in the center of the room and looked about. A deep sigh escaped him. He glanced at the clock and stole into the kitchen to inspect the beans.

Before he reached the oven, he heard the sharp knock of hard knuckles on the outside door of the apartment. The back of Battle's neck, being the only part of him that was not covered with some kind of make-up, turned white.

For a long moment, he jittered between the door into the living room and the oven. The living room won. He stepped inside on tiptoe and took one final peak at himself in the mirror, sighed deeply—shivered as he shook his head and advanced toward the door. The knocking came again—louder.

"Buck up, old chap. Keep your nerve. You are now the Master—the Master Spy, do you hear? Buck up and keep a cool head. Do not let them perceive that you are nervous. Hold yourself ready for any emergency. Now you must open the door."

The knock sounded a third time and the door trembled beneath those heavy strokes.

"One, two, three!" Battle counted to himself.

He took just long enough after that to breathe a prayer and a sigh, then he turned the key and boldly threw the door open wide.

For an instant, the dark hole that was the yawning doorway seemed filled with ghastly faces. There was one man directly before Battle who leaped across the threshold and stood there, grinning horribly.

He was a hammered-down sort of brute

with shoulders almost as broad as they were high from the floor. His face appeared perfectly flat, with chin, gaping mouth, nose and eyebrows all on the same plane.

"Oh, I say," Battle exploded, shrinking back from shock.

The other three ugly, menacing brutes, dressed in ill-fitting Yank uniforms, crowded in behind. The squat leader pushed Battle before him and the last man in, a bent, spidery sort with long arms, short legs and only half a face because his chin was gone, closed the door behind him.

Battle shrank still farther away so as to be as much out of reach as possible. The leader strode after him. He stuck out a hand that was three times the width of one of Battle's.

Battle was taking his part. He must act like G-8, although the thought of touching one of these foul-looking beasts gave him a new attack of the jitters.

The powerful paw closed over his and held on. Battle was jerked forward and the automatic that he had counted on not a little was ripped from its holster.

"So you are de *verdammt* one, G-8?" the leader barked.

He released him now that the gun was

gone. Battle was making a terrific fight to keep hold of himself. He bowed.

"Yes, sir," he stammered. "I—I am G-8. What do you gentlemen want?"

The other three joined in the laughter of their leader.

"We want you," the squat one rasped. "You are coming with us—to *Herr Stahlmaske*. He is ready to use you for testing his *Loscher* machine."

At a nod from the leader, the other three leaped forward. Battle tried to get away from them, but he was snatched into the center of the room and half dragged toward the door, calling:

"I say, look here, you can't do this!"

Suddenly, the leader blocked the way of the others.

"Wait," he ordered. "*Eine minute*. There is something *nicht gut heir*. Let him go!"

Battle stood shaking a little before him. The wicked eyes of the brute man burned into his.

"You are *nicht* G-8," he snorted. "Dere is trickery here. I giff you one chance to tell. Who are you?"

"I," he snapped, "am G-8." His fists doubled in a pitiful effort at bravado but he was game. "Who dares say I am not the Master Spy?"

"I say you are not G-8," the leader roared. "*Und* I say that you are a *verdammt* liar."

The huge right paw of the leader zipped through the air in front of Battle's face and smacked him full with the open palm, hurling him backward. He didn't go down, but landed against the side of the room. He braced himself with head still reeling and lunged at the brute.

His fists were flying, awkwardly, into the face of the leader, but bouncing off like pebbles tossed against the face of a cliff. The brute was laughing at him and making no attempt to protect himself.

Desperately, Battle fought on. Righteous anger welled up in him and spurred him on to try the impossible.

The brute leader seemed to grow tired of his joke. His left hand shot out and grasped Battle by the front of his loose uniform coat and jerked him nearer. The huge right fist shot across the intervening space and landed between Battle's eyes.

Stars blinked for only the briefest instant and then everything went black for the master of make-up.

Men talked while consciousness returned.

He heard the four brutes in far-off mumbling.

"The *verdammt* one and his assistants should be back soon," he heard the leader say. "Vee will catch them as they come in the door. Two of us on each side and wait there. We wait until all three are in the room and then—"

Battle was lying on the floor. He could not move his arms or legs for they were tied. He tried to cry out but realized for the first time that breathing was difficult because of something that was tied about his head.

He strained at the bindings, but the ropes only cut into his flesh more deeply.

The leader's voice lowered.

"Silence! Listen. They are coming now in their planes!"

A hush fell over the room. The only sound Battle could hear was the ever-increasing drone of Hissos. In spite of the mass of cloth covering his head, he could make out the three engines.

"Ach, gut," the Hun said. "Now they come to land."

The sound of the engines died. Very faintly, Battle could hear the whistle of wind tearing through wires and over wings.

G-8 and Nippy and Bull were landing. They were walking right into this trap.

He struggled with renewed vigor to get free but his efforts were in vain. There came the rumble of wheels and skids as the three Spads landed outside and motors blurped again, jerking the three ships to the end hangar tarmac.

They would be getting out now. Battle was frantic but helpless. He tried to make a sound with his mouth, and when that failed, he found he could pound with his heels on the floor.

There came a curse in German and the soft padding of heavy feet toward him. Outside, he heard G-8's voice speaking to his mechanic the instant after the engines ceased to idle. He thought it could hear their boots striking the hard apron outside as they walked toward the apartment door where the Hun brutes lurked.

Battle kicked with all his might to warn them. It was all that he could do. Something like a sledge hammer struck him at the side of the head. It might have been the toe of the leader's boot, or a club. Battle didn't know, for it blasted him into unconsciousness again.

CHAPTER SIX
Bull Cleans House

G-8 climbed out of his cockpit and stretched.
Nippy and Bull gathered about him in the
darkness.

"G-8," Bull said seriously, "have you any
idea what made those engines stop at
Nancy?"

G-8 frowned and gave a significant nod
at the mechanic sergeant who had come to
take care of his Spad. He called him over.

"Sergeant," he asked, "have you had any
engines on test here tonight?"

The sergeant looked puzzled for a moment and then he nodded down the dark
tarmac.

"You can hear 'em running now, sir," he
said.

"Yes," G-8 agreed, "that's right. Have
they been running like that all evening?"

"I'll say so, sir," the sergeant nodded
savagely. "They could have picked nights
that would suit me better. I've had a head-

ache all day big enough for a hippopotomus.
Warming engines wasn't so bad because
they'd stop once in a while, but those motors on test—honest, sir, I'm about to go
nuts."

"They haven't stopped once in the last
three hours?" G-8 ventured.

"The last three hours, sir? They haven't
stopped since they started before mess
tonight."

"Good," G-8 nodded.

The sergeant stared, wide-eyed, and his
mouth dropped open.

G-8 turned to Nippy and Bull, and together they walked toward the trap waiting to be sprung on them.

"That settles one thing," G-8 said when
he was out of earshot of the mechanics.
"*Stahlmaske* has his headquarters over in
the Black Forest, in the general region of
Nancy. We felt the force there, but they
didn't get it here."

"You mean," Nippy demanded, "that
they've got a device that will stop airplane engines that are as far away as
Nancy is from the Black Forest?"

"I wouldn't bet they didn't have," G-8
advised. "And if that's all they've got, we'll
be lucky. I wonder what the force of the
apparatus is within a few hundred yards."

Suddenly, Nippy and G-8 stopped simultaneously. Bull stopped two paces ahead of them and turned.

"What's the idea of you—" the big fellow began but he got no farther because a low warning hiss for silence came from G-8.

"Hey!" Nippy whispered. "Do you smell something burning?"

"Yes," G-8 nodded. "Something's burning in our kitchen and I'm sure I heard a thudding sound, just a moment ago."

"I don't see anything to get excited about in that," Bill rumbled.

"Shut up, you big ox," Nippy breathed. "Think this over. Did you ever catch Battle letting something burn?"

"Holy Herring! No, come to think of it," Bull agreed.

"That and the pounding in there is what started me thinking," G-8 admitted. "It seems strange to smell the odor of burned cooking coming from Battle's kitchen. He's always so careful about things like that."

The Master Spy walked a little nearer and stopped again.

"There's something phoney going on," Nippy ventured. "Either Battle isn't there or he's too sick to look after things in the kitchen."

"Look at the windows. The heavy shades are drawn. Never saw him do that before," G-8 said.

"Well," Bull growled. "What are we waiting out here for? Let's go in and see what's wrong."

He started, but G-8 caught his arm and drew him back.

"Not so fast," he whispered. "We'll take a little look around first. Let's try the kitchen and see if we can slip in there."

Around at the other side of the apartment section of the hangar they found the kitchen door locked.

"Looks like Battle's locked himself in because he was afraid of something," Nippy guessed.

"I don't know what you birds are talking about," Bull snorted. "What would Battle be afraid of, inside the apartment?"

"Maybe," G-8 ventured, "if you'll quiet down, we'll find out. Come on. Quiet now, through the storage end, and we'll have a look from that door."

"You mean through the keyhole?" Nippy asked.

"Yes," G-8 hissed, leading the way through the hangar.

"But there's a guard over the keyhole," Nippy objected.

"I know, but I think I can work it back without making any noise."

"Better let me try it," Nippy suggested. "I'm used to light-fingered stuff with my magic tricks."

They had reached the door in question. G-8 nodded assent.

Nippy produced a small piece of wire and went to work. In less than two minutes he was peering through the hole that he had opened. He drew back as though someone from the living room had jabbed him with a hat pin.

"Jumping Jupiter!" he gasped. "Wait until you see what I saw. There are four of the ugliest-looking things I ever saw in my life, crouched, two on each side of the opposite door, waiting for us to come in that way. Somebody with a uniform that fits him like a circus tent is tied up over by the fireplace. I can't see who it is because there's a blanket tied over his head."

G-8 drew him away and was staring through the small opening.

"I'll give odds of three to one that it's Battle," he offered. "Or at least it was Battle. He isn't moving."

"You mean they killed Battle?" Bull hissed. "Listen, I kid that guy a lot, but if

74

they killed him, I'll break every bone in their bodies. Ugly? They'll be ugly when I get through with them. Let me have a look, will you, G-8?"

Bull took one look and leaped up.

"Listen," he announced in a close whisper, "there's only one way to beat these birds. We've got to surprise them. This door is locked, so we've got to break it down as we go and keep on bucking the line. You birds follow your interference. And this is going to be some interference."

"Right," G-8 agreed, drawing his automatic.

Bull stepped back from the door. G-8 crouched beside him.

"We'll go through together," he said. "Nip, you clean up what we miss."

"Yeah," the terrier ace hissed. "I sure will."

"One—two—three!" Bull breathed.

Bull and G-8 charged with heads together and right shoulders jutting forward. Nippy tore in behind them, pushing with his hands against their hips.

There was a sharp report of wood and metal shattering. The door went down before them like the side of a child's playhouse and Bull plowed on, with G-8 a close second and Nippy running beside him.

All four of the brutes heard and saw their danger at the same time. Their moves were ill-timed and jumbled.

The squat leader drew a gun as Bull came at him, head down. The brute's hand moved with lightning speed, and before G-8 could little more than realize it, he had swung the gun round and was leveling it straight for Bull's middle.

The Master Spy tried to get in a shot from his already drawn Colt automatic, but all was a mad mass of movement and Bull was between him and that squat figure.

Two things happened so closely together that G-8 wasn't sure of the exact outcome until he saw it definitely.

The brute man had brought his gun up and had pulled the trigger, but the lunging football star had also moved so fast that G-8 didn't quite follow him with his eyes.

Bull's body above his waist had tipped back, and his right kicking foot had swung up like a high-speed, murderous pendulum. G-8 couldn't see what that tried and true toe of Bull's had struck, but he saw the gun of the brute crash against the ceiling and fall. He heard a scream of pain.

The two brutes from the other side of

the door leaped at Bull, but the big fellow dropped to a crouched position once more, ducked to the left to let them slip by and hurled a right and a left into the flat face of the leader.

The left sent him off his balance. The right snapped the head back on the thick neck, and with glazed eyes the leader crashed to the floor and lay still.

G-8 fired his automatic with the muzzle not three feet from the side of another contorted one who was in the very act of sending a bullet for Bull's head.

G-8's gun exploded with a deafening roar and blasted a second time. The brute at the end of the muzzle jerked, flopped and hit the floor with a sodden thud.

G-8 swerved his gun to fire at another, but a third brute was already charging from the side with upraised arm and a wicked knife in his hand.

Bull made a frantic effort to reach him. It seemed too late to call out and warn the Master Spy of his danger. Nippy was already taking care of the situation. His slim, wiry body was flying through the air straight for the running feet of the surprise attacker.

Bull let out a bellowing cry of warning, and struck. His blow landed just in time to change the aim of the knife hand so that the blade barely ripped through G-8's coat and pricked his skin.

The human beast was far from knocked out. He was on his feet instantly, the most powerful of all the four brutes. As he rose, he snatched at Nippy's shoulder and jerked the terrier ace upward. The knife blade gleamed.

Nippy whirled in a frantic effort to jerk free of the murderous grasp. He succeeded in part, and let fly with a right that landed full in the stomach of the brute.

Again and again G-8 pulled the trigger of his automatic. Lead spat from the muzzle and slammed into the living room wall. The brute had leaped to the side and spun Nippy about to use him as a shield.

Bull was there, his great hands closing on the German. The brute dropped Nippy to fight off Bull. The knife which had not yet touched Nippy came slashing down at Bull. The big fellow ducked in and caught the wrist on his shoulder. He seized that wrist in his left hand and there was a terrific struggle. Bull gave a sharp twist of the other's arm and brought up his right to the jaw. The knife thudded to the floor.

The brute made a wild attempt to pick

up the knife, but Bull kicked it away with a growl and let go again with rights and lefts.

For a half minute, G-8 and Nippy watched from the side. Bull was having no easy time of it, but he was doing a thorough job, cleaning house with his last brute.

Suddenly, Bull charged with head down. He picked up the brute and tossed him with terrific force against the end of the living room.

The flying body made a sickly sound when it struck the masonry of the fireplace, head first. It slumped, the head bashed in, not three feet from where Battle's body lay.

All hands were working now to free Battle. Bull ripped the blanket from his head and Nippy and G-8 cut the ropes that bound his hands and feet. All three stared in astonishment when Battle's face, made up to look like G-8's, was uncovered. They next took stock of his wounds. He had an ugly bruise at his temple where the leader had kicked him. The middle of his face was swollen a little, too. He was out cold.

Nippy and Bull worked to revive the English manservant while G-8 called guards and ordered the bodies to be taken out. As they picked up the brute leader, he showed signs of life.

"Keep him on ice for a firing squad," G-8 ordered.

Battle was coming around. He opened his eyes and blinked about from one face to the other.

"Oh, I say!" he gasped. "Was it a dream, or have you gentlemen been calfing me again?"

"Kidding, you mean," Nippy cut in. "Got your milk animals mixed up."

"Oh yes, of course!" Battle groaned, sitting up.

"What," Bull panted, "gives you the idea that we've been kidding you?"

"Perhaps I'm a bit off my bean as you might say, sir," Battle blinked, rubbing his head. "But it doesn't make much sense, you know. There were, as I remember, four gentlemen—oh, horrible-looking specimens—who entered and demanded to know where you were, G-8, sir."

Battle stared about and his roving eyes landed first on the pool of blood left by the brute whom Bull had thrown against the masonry.

"Oh, look here, did someone cut his finger, or—"

"Or!" Nippy nodded. "Those horrible-looking birds you're talking about have been generally cleaned up—mostly by Bull." He turned to the big fellow with a grin. "As a house cleaner, fella, I'll bet you'll make some ragman a nice wife. You don't leave the place very tidy, but you sure do get rid of a lot of junk in a hurry."

"Alright," Bull growled. "Laugh, squirt. I got my mind on serious things. What I'm trying to figure out is why Battle is made up to look like you, G-8."

"I've been a little curious about that myself," the Master Spy confessed.

They helped Battle over to the davenport where he sat down with a relieved groan like an old sheep dog dropping down beside the stove.

"I trust," Battle pleaded, "that I haven't given offense, sir."

G-8 smiled.

"Not to me, you haven't, Battle," he told him. "But from the looks of the treatment you got I'd say that you seemed offensive to someone."

"Eh?" Battle blinked. "Oh, yes sir! I certainly was on the offensive!"

"O. K.," G-8 laughed. "Have it any way you like, Battle. We can sure tell that you got socked a couple of times but you haven't—"

"Oh, but I say, sir," Battle cut in, "I didn't get socked twice. "Really I didn't. The blighter struck me only once with his fist." He pointed to the bruised temple. "This, I believe, was delivered with the toe of his boot."

"Boy, that was clever ducking," Bull observed. "You only let him hit you once with his fist, eh? Sort of walked right into a good, swift kick to change the monotony?"

"Oh, no, indeed," Battle hurried. "Not at all. You see, sir, I was bound and lying on the floor as a result of being knocked cockeyed. I was just about coming to my senses once more—no wisecracks, if you please, about my senses—when I heard you coming and tried to signal you by thumping my feet upon the floor."

"That was what we heard," G-8 nodded to the others.

"Righto!" Battle beamed. "I'm so glad I helped matters! But as I was saying, I was signaling when *bang, biff* and by Jove—I felt something like a sledge hammer battering through the blanket into my temple. Then as you might say, sleep came to a weary soul—er—rather definitely—if you gather what I mean."

By now Nippy was convulsed, Bull was

shaking and heaving with laughter, and G-8 was chuckling.

"Oh, but I say!" Battle chirped on. "You're all waiting for me to tell you how I thought of putting this face on, aren't you, eh? Well, you see the bounder that called to see if you were in, G-8, spoke with a marked German accent. I suspected that something was afoot at once and I said to myself, 'Battle, you haven't done much for the master and he's done much for you, so you'd better have a go at impersonating him and taking the—er—spot for him if there is trouble.' So"—Battle shrugged his slim shoulders from which hung the ill-fitting uniform—"I just did it. It really didn't come out so badly as I feared."

G-8 was suddenly grave.

"You mean, Battle," he demanded, "that you were going to take anything for me?"

"Well, you see, sir, begging your pardon, I thought I might—"

Battle got no farther. G-8 threw one arm around him and patted one of those slim shoulders affectionately.

"You old son of a gun!" the Master Spy exploded. "Don't you know it was just like throwing yourself under a train to take my place?"

"A train?" Battle repeated blankly. "I say, look here—I didn't see any train."

Nippy and Bull burst out with a fresh roar of laughter.

"Shut up," G-8 barked. "We've all kidded Battle enough. He's got a lot of guts and he deserves some respect around here."

"Oh, but I say!" Battle said, blinking. "Kidding and laughter I don't mind, sir. It's much better than having persons angry all of the time." He straightened. "You know," he said, "for many years I've been a bit of a joke. They used to call me 'Balmy' Battle, sir, because I was a bit slow in catching on—if you see what I mean. But I don't mind, sir. I rather fancy it, you know. Sort of makes me feel as though I'm worth something—keeping people in good humor and whatnot."

There was a moment of awkward silence during which Battle sighed. "I'm afraid I've proven to myself that I'm not much of a fighter sir."

"Baloney," Bull roared. "You have the most important requisite for a fighter. You have courage, fella, and I'm all for you. Just to prove it to you, I'm going to get the next meal and wash the dishes for you while you take it easy."

A heavy knock on the door transformed

the interior of the apartment to a place of silence. G-8 rose from the davenport where he had been beside Battle and strode toward the door.

"Hey," Bull hissed, "take it easy! It might be some more of those birds."

"Don't worry," the Master Spy flung over his shoulder. "I'm set."

His right hand had dropped to his holster. He had his automatic half out when his left hand turned the latch of the door. He flung it open and stepped back.

A lone figure peered in out of the dark. G-8 let his gun fall at once, for this was a young flying officer, dressed in his best O. D. uniform and blinking in the light that sprayed through the doorway. He had a newspaper-wrapped package under his arm.

"Come in, won't you, Lieutenant?" G-8 offered cordially.

"Thanks," the other saluted. "I'm Lieutenant Farber from the 46th observation squadron." He stepped across the threshold and G-8 closed the door behind him. "A few days ago an enemy plane dropped this package of personal effects on our field." He handed it to the Master Spy. "I'm down here on a four-days leave, and I thought you'd know what to do with it. I believe you were flying the plane that this man dropped out of."

G-8 took the package and turned it over. His eyes fell on a typewritten note pinned to the German newspaper.

Inclosed you will find personal effects of Captain Billings whose body was recently discovered.

Lieutenant Farber saluted and turned toward the door.

"I'll be running along, if you don't mind, sir," he said.

"Of course," G-8 agreed. "You'll want to make as much of your four days as you can. Thanks a lot."

The package fell partly open as G-8 laid it out on the table. A pocket mirror and a small Bible rolled out. Nippy and Bull were investigating the other effects on their own hook.

G-8 stood soberly looking on. Suddenly, he reached forward and picked up the old German newspaper that had served as a wrapping. His eyes flashed across the page and he tensed. An exclamation escaped him.

"Look here!" he cried. "This is a Freiburg paper of several days ago. We're in luck! Listen to this."

CHAPTER SEVEN
Special Mission

G-8 began reading from a lead article on the rumpled front page of the newspaper.

ELECTRICAL WIZARD ABDUCTED

WAS REPUTED SECRETLY EXPERIMENTING WITH WIRELESS BEAM

The entire section of the country about Freiburg is now being searched by police for the eminent *Herr Doktor* Frielinger who vanished from his home at 32 Ahornbaum Strasse shortly after ten o'clock last night. According to the story told by *Frau* Frielinger, who is reported to be suffering injuries met at the hands of the abductors, their home was entered about ten o'clock by three horrible-looking men. One of them, who seemed to be the leader, wore a sort of steel helmet that covered his entire head and neck to the shoulders. It was he, *Frau* Frielinger says, who struck her, knocking her senseless. When she regained consciousness, she found that her husband, *Herr Doktor* Frielinger, was gone and her ten-year-old son Emil lay unconscious on the dining room floor, his face horribly mangled. The boy is now in the Freiburg Hospital with an even chance to live. Police and military officials are investigating the story of *Frau* Frielinger.

G-8 lowered the paper and turned to Battle, smiling significantly.

"Well, Battle," he said. "Do you feel like doing a job?"

"Job, sir?" Battle asked.

"Yes," G-8 nodded. "I want to look like someone else, before the night is over."

"You mean," Bull demanded, "you're going over into Germany just because you get a chance to read a week-old newspaper from a dump like Freiburg?"

"You seem to get the general idea," G-8 admitted.

He held the paper up to the light so that he could see through it.

"What are you doing, look for code writing?" Nippy asked.

G-8 shook his head.

"Hardly," he said. "You see, I want to take this clipping along with me." He smiled a little. "So I can have some reading to pass away the time with if I should get stuck in jail in Germany. I'm going to tear out an article on the other side of the same page of the newspaper. This one will do nicely. It has a list of names of children who assisted in a patriotic parade."

He began tearing the sheet in a jagged half circle.

"I still don't get it," Bull persisted. "What is there about the abduction of a guy by the name of *Doktor* Flimdigger, or whatever you called him, that makes you think you've got to go over into Germany right away?"

"Maybe, you big ox," Nippy cut in, "if you'd listened to what G-8 read, you'd know more about it. Didn't you hear him say anything about a guy with a steel helmet?"

"No," the big fellow admitted. "Does it say that?"

G-8 held the clipping out and pointed with his finger.

"Read it yourself," he suggested.

Bull stared.

"Holy Herring!" he said. "That's right. Then that ties up with everything, doesn't it?"

"Pretty nearly," the Master Spy admitted. "The way I have the thing figured out is this: *Herr Stahlmaske* was working secretly with some kind of a beam that would do harm to planes and pilots. He had reached the point where he could conk one of our engines if he was close enough. He knew of *Herr Doktor* Frielinger's work with the wireless beam. Perhaps he was associated with it at one time. Anyway, he decided to go over and take the doctor and also the invention. I've heard of *Doktor* Frielinger before. He's noted as an electrical wizard, second to none. I don't mind telling you I'm a little worried about his beam falling into the hands of this maniac, *Stahlmaske*."

"Gee," Nippy cut in excitedly, I'll bet the force that stopped those engines at Nancy was Frielinger's beam."

G-8 nodded in grave assent.

"There's no doubt about it," he agreed. "That's why I'm anxious, now that I've got this lead, to go over and start working at once."

"One thing I can't see," Bull insisted stubbornly, "is how you expect to get anywhere on it if the police and military forces in their own country can't find out where he is. You've got to go over as a spy, which means that you'll have one strike on you to start with."

"Granted," the Master Spy admitted. "But did you notice this?"

G-8 read again the last sentence of the article.

Police and military police are investigating the story of *Frau* Frielinger.

He looked up.

"You see," he explained, "there seems to be some doubt in their minds as to the authenticity of her story."

"Yeah," Nippy admitted, "I was thinking of that, too. Anyone would think she was lying to cover up her husband."

"That," G-8 said, "is one thing that possibly will hinder the German authorities in finding out what has actually happened to *Herr Doktor* Frielinger."

"Jumping Jupiter!" Nippy exploded. "Can it be possible that the German command doesn't *know* that there's such a guy as *Herr Stahlmaske?*"

"He's probably on record somewhere," G-8 centured, "because he was burned so badly that he must have gone to a hospital. But the chances are that since he's gotten out, he's been more or less forgotten by the officials. I'll gamble that they wouldn't put any stock in his importance. However, I'd be willing to bet my life against roast duck for Christmas dinner that you'll find *Herr Doktor* Frielinger a prisoner not a hundred yards away from where you'll find *Stahlmaske.*"

The Master Spy began pawing through his wardrobe of disguise clothing.

"Here," he said, laying out a suit of German cut that was a dark gray in color. "This ought to go well with a scholarly-looking man, don't you think, Battle?"

The English manservant got up from the davenport and nodded.

"Yes, sir," he said, "I think it would do admirably, sir, for one of that stamp. You wish to be made up, then, as a professor or teacher?"

"Not quite as strong as that," the Master Spy said. "Let's say I'm about fifty years old and wear glasses. I'll pick those out myself. I've almost white hair and a white moustache. Not the Kaiser kind but quite ordinary, rather close-cropped."

Battle bowed, taking out his make-up kit.

"It will be a pleasure."

G-8 was already reclining in one of the big chairs with a towel back of his head. Battle went to work. When he had finished, G-8 donned the business suit. He glanced at the tailor's mark along the inside pocket and saw that it was from a modest custom tailor's establishment in Berlin. When he had passed his own inspection before the mirror, he turned to his Battle Aces.

"Bull," he ordered. "You go and arrange for that German Rumpler two-seater plane in hangar 3 to be fueled and warmed. Then get into a set of German flying togs and be ready for a night flight."

"Jumping Jupiter, aren't you going to let me take you this time?" Nippy asked.

"No, I'm going to give Bull a turn at it," G-8 smiled. "Besides, this is supposed to be an authentic flight, and Bull's build makes him look more like a real German than you do."

Bull grinned at the terrier ace.

"There, squirt," he said. "That will hold you for a while."

The big fellow stalked triumphantly out on the tarmac.

"Nippy, you can help me with the papers I'll need," G-8 said. "I want to go at this thing very carefully. Until I reach Freiburg, my name will be"—he glanced at the clipping—"Otto Hempel."

"I've heard of writers getting names out of telephone directories," Nippy said, "but I never heard of a spy casually picking a name for himself out of a week-old newspaper clipping."

G-8 smiled.

"I have a reason for that," he said. "Look, here in this list of names on the back of the clipping. You see, there was a girl, Augustine Hempel, who was the leader of the patriotic parade. Strangely enough she lives at number 20 Ahornbaum Strasse. That puts her on the even side of the street, if you remember, with 32 Ahornbaum Strasse, the home of *Herr Doktor* Frielinger. That's where I expect to go as soon as I make sure the coast is clear."

"Jumping Jupiter!" Nippy exclaimed. "You think of everything, don't you?"

"I try to, but sometimes I fall way short," the Master Spy admitted. "How are you coming with those papers?"

"I'll have them ready in a couple of

minutes," Nippy assured him. "You get on your flying suit."

G-8 was selecting a pair of glasses for himself. He found a pair of horn-rimmed spectacles that suited him. Then he got into the German flying suit that he had selected for himself. As he finished, Nippy handed him the papers.

The engine of the Rumpler roared outside and Bull came in to announce that he was ready. G-8 gathered up the few necessities for his mission and climbed into the rear cockpit.

"Got enough gas to make Kehl on the Rhine?" he asked.

"I thought you were going to—" Bull began. Then he nodded. "Sure," he said. "That's across the Rhine from Freiburg, isn't it? I've got a half tank on this truck but I'll have to stop on the way back."

"All right," G-8 nodded. He handed the big fellow a map. "I've marked a field outside of Kehl. I'll get there in time to catch the morning train for Freiburg, if they're still running on the old schedule."

For two hours they flew through the night, dead on their course. The sky was thick with clouds when they left Le Bourget but in the mountain regions as they crossed the lines, it began to clear. Stars came out and hung above them. After a few minutes they could see, straight ahead and slightly to the right, the higher peaks of the Black Forest.

G-8 spoke to Bull through the tube:

"We ought to be pretty close to that field now. When you go down, drop a flare and land close by."

He heard the big fellow explode, "Huh? Holy Herring, what's the idea, G-8? Have you gone nutty? I can see a light down there by that field. There's a house near there. Looks like somebody's carrying a lantern."

"That's all the more reason," G-8 told him, "why you should go down openly. You want to make that farmer down there certain that everything is O. K. with our landing. If he's got any sense, he'll be sure that an enemy spy wouldn't dare land in the light of a flare."

"I'll bet that you'd kiss the Kaiser," Bull croaked, "if you thought it would help turn suspicion away from you."

"I would," G-8 laughed, "if it would help win the war. Come on, there's the field down there now. Drop a flare and get ready to land. The minute I hop out, you turn around and shove off again."

"You certainly put yourself in some swell jams," Bull complained, shaking his big head. "But anything you say goes, chief."

Below and behind, a flare plopped out and began drifting down at the end of its little parachute, brilliantly illuminating the space beneath the Rumpler two-seater with a unnatural, white light.

Bull dropped the nose of his Rumpler and cut the gun so that the motor idled restlessly. He lost one, two thousand feet, now three. In the last five hundred he circled and came in over the boundary to set his ship down.

G-8 watched the light that had been moving at the side of the field. Now that they were closer, he could see that the light was motionless, located between two buildings—a house and a barn. He glanced at his wrist watch and found it was well past four in the morning. This was a German peasant farmer out doing his chores.

The Master Spy spoke softly through the tube to Bull.

"Give me a chance to take off my flying togs before you pull out. I'll say *auf wiedersehn* when I'm ready."

"O.K.," Bull agreed, centering all his intention now upon landing in the little field. They jolted to a stop over semi-rough ground. G-8 got out instantly and began taking off the captured German flying suit, helmet, and goggles. He was still watching that light over near the buildings at the side of the field. It was moving toward him with the rapid, regular motion of a man's walk. This, then, was the German peasant farmer coming out to meet their ship.

The Master Spy stuffed the flying togs in the rear cockpit, gave a soft, *"Auf wiedersehn"* to Bull, and stepped out of the way so that his severe gray clothing would remain clean.

The Rumpler motor roared. Bull was rapidly taxiing down the field for a full length take-off. G-8 pretended to be absorbed in the turn he made, but out of the corner of his eye he was watching the swinging lantern as it came closer.

In the next instant, a voice out of the darkness gutturalled:

"Was ist?"

G-8 turned immediately. He knew the light was shining upon him, so he bowed stiffly.

"Wie gehts," he greeted. "Has his Excellency, the general, arrived yet?"

By now the farmer had come up to confront him.

"Bitte," he said, speaking loudly so he could be heard over the thunderous roar of Bull's plane. "I do not understand, *mein Herr*. There is no general here."

"You mean," G-8 demanded, "that this is not the Kehl airdrome?"

"Ach nein," the farmer said, "I am very sorry, *mein Herr,* but you are more than twenty-five kilometers from the Kehl airdrome. I am Hans Neidderheim and this is my farm. I fear your plane has landed in the wrong place."

"Ach du Lieber," G-8 cried.

He knew that Bull had already taken the air, could tell by the free drone of his engine that he had started on his homeward trip, but nevertheless he whirled around and started to run after the plane, waving his arms in movements that he knew Bull couldn't possibly see in the darkness. The farmer followed him, waving his lantern but Bull kept on going.

"I am sorry," the farmer apologized. "I should have let you know sooner, but *Himmel,* I did not know that you were at the wrong place."

G-8 smiled.

"It is quite all right," he said. "There is no hurry. Perhaps you could drive me to

Kehl so I can procure transportation to the airdrome."

"*Jawohl*," the farmer beamed, "it would be a pleasure. I will tell Lena to milk the cows while I go."

The farmer hurried away with his lantern, calling his wife. G-8 followed.

Lena was a perfect match for Hans. Like him, she was comfortably stout and in spite of the war, jovial.

"*Ach,* Hans," she cried, "You have company for breakfast."

G-8 bowed.

"*Bitte, Frau* Neidderheim," he said, "I regret that I dare not take the time to accept your most kind invitation. I am sure I shall be missing an excellent breakfast."

"*Ja,*" the husband grunted. "Do not interrupt the gentleman. He has more important work to do than wait until you cook breakfast." Neidderheim's chest swelled out a little. "I am to drive him to Kehl at once," he announced. "You will finish milking the cows, Lena, while I hitch up the horses."

Frau Neidderheim heaved a sigh of disappointment and went obediently into the barn while G-8 followed the farmer into the stable. He was in the act of helping

100

him hitch the old raw-boned horses to the only wagon the farmer owned, when from down the road there came the roar of a swiftly-driven car.

The Master Spy steeled himself even before the car had reached the group of buildings. It scuffed to a stop in the loose gravel of the road and he saw that there were two German officers, both hurriedly climbing out of the front seat. But the Master Spy made no attempt to run.

In the light of the lantern one of the *offiziers* was demanding importantly, "Did anybody get out of that plane that just landed here?"

The German farmer opened his mouth to speak.

CHAPTER EIGHT
The Spy at Work

It was plainly evident that an explanation to these investigators was unavoidable. It was up to G-8 to make that explanation as convincing as possible.

Before the farmer could do more than open his mouth, the Master Spy smiled, bowed, and stepped forward.

"Bitte, herr offizieren," he said in a deep, dignified voice. "It was I who got out of the plane that landed."

For an instant the Hunn *offiziers* halted, mouths agape. The smaller and apparently more important one caught his breath first and blurted out:

"So you admit you are the one?"

"Admit?" G-8 repeated questioningly. He moved toward them casually. "I'm afraid, *mein herren,* that I see nothing to admit."

The two *offiziers* strode up to the disguised Master Spy. Now the larger Hun spoke.

"Mein herr," he said, "we have been sent to investigate the landing of a plane a few minutes ago in this vicinity. It is suspected of being an enemy plane landing a spy."

"An enemy plane?" G-8 repeated. *"Ach, das ist gut."* He turned to the farmer who had left his half-hitched horse and come to join him. *"Herr* Neidderheim, I believe you said that was your name," G-8 began. "Did you see the plane that I got out of?"

"Jawohl," the farmer nodded. "I saw it very clearly, *mein herr."*

"Perhaps you would tell these *offiziers*

what you saw on it," the Master Spy continued. "Did you see colored circles in the light of your latern or did you see black crosses?"

"I saw black crosses, of course, *mein herren*," the farmer said. "There was a black cross on the side of the plane beside where the operator sat and there was also another black cross back on the up-right part of the tail."

Neiderheim looked a little fearfully at the *offiziers*.

"*Bitte*, is there anything wrong?" he asked timidly. "Am I in trouble for permitting this gentleman to land on my field?"

"I can explain matters very simply," G-8 cut in. "I am *Herr* Hempel, flown here on special secret mission from Metz. My pilot and I became confused in the darkness. He was going to land me at the Kehl airdrome which *Herr* Neidderheim tells me is far on the other side of the city. Before I understood the mistake, the plane had taken off once more. *Herr* Neidderheim has kindly offered to drive me to Kehl. As you can see, he was hitching up the horses when you gentlemen arrived."

G-8 glanced at the farmer and the horses and wobbly wagon and then at the headlights of the car shining some yards away.

"I presume, now that you *offiziers* have come, I might ride to Kehl with you," he said, "so *Herr* Neidderheim will not be inconvenienced, *nicht wahr?*"

This last stroke of the Master Spy completely disarmed the investigating *offiziers*. The shorter one took command once more with that same important swagger.

"Bitte, mein Herr," he said, "it will be a pleasure to take you to Kehl with us. We ask your pardon for suspecting you, but of course, as a matter of form, we must demand to see your papers."

G-8 bowed, drew back the coat of his suit so that the flashlight held in the *offizier's* hand shone for an instant on the Berlin tailor's label inside and drew out the papers that Nippy had fixed for him.

Both *offiziers* made brief inspections of the papers and handed them back to the Master Spy.

"Are we ready to depart now, gentlemen?" G-8 asked.

"Jawohl," the Huns nodded.

"Und may I," G-8 said, turning and holding out his hand to the farmer, "offer my sincere gratitude for your hospitality and aid, *Herr* Neidderheim." He appeared to be in no hurry to leave. "Perhaps before I go I should help you unharness the horse."

"Ach du Lieber, nein," the farmer objected. "Already you have your hands dirty
enough."

"Very well, then," G-8 bowed. *"Auf
wiedersehen und* once more, *danke schon."*

But as the Master Spy turned he wasn't
yet sure whether these two *offiziers* really
trusted him. They had both been sitting
in the front seat when they arrived. Now,
in another half minute, when they reached
the car, he would know for sure, from the
seat that they offered him. If it were to be
the front seat—

He kept his gentlemanly bearing even
as he halted there, waiting upon the wishes
of the other two. With light bag in hand,
he stood where he could easily step through
either front or back door when opened.

"Where, *mein herren,"* he asked, "would
it be most convenient to have me sit?"

The tall *offizier* opened the rear door
and nodded.

"You may have the back seat all to yourself, *mein herr,"* he announced. The Master
Spy knew then that he had won his point.

G-8 bowed again and stepped in and the
door was slammed shut by the *offizier* who
climbed into the front seat. The tall one
slipped behind the wheel, turned the car
about, and headed for town.

Daylight came rapidly as they drove the short distance. The gray light showed the buildings along the main street when the short *offizier* turned in the front seat to ask of G-8:

"Did you wish to have us take you to the airdrome or call a taxi to take you there?" he asked.

"The airdrome?" G-8 repeated absent-mindedly. "Oh, yes, the airdrome. I had almost forgotten. *Nein.* I was only going to land there in the plane and then hire a car to bring me into town."

The Master Spy glanced at the office buildings on either side. There was one just opposite, and glancing over the top of his thick glasses for an instant, he saw the name on the building.

SCHACHT

"Bitte," he said, looking about through his glasses once more in a bewildered fashion. "I have an early appointment with a high official in the Schacht Building. My eyes are not so good in this light."

"The Schacht Building?" the short one said. "We just passed it in the last block."

"Ach, I am sorry," G-8 apologized. I must not put you to any more trouble—except for one thing."

The car drew up to the curb.

"I am here on a mission of greatest secrecy," G-8 went on in a hushed voice. "It is most important to His Excellency, the Chief of Staff, that my visit be unmentioned." He leaned very close to the two. "May I be assured of your silence, *mein herren*, for our *Kaiser?*"

By now, both Huns were both sitting stiff, with chests out. Heads nodded in the affirmative.

"*Jawohl,*" they agreed in an awed whisper.

"*Aber,*" added the driver, "I will turn the car around *und* take you back to the Schacht building."

"Better," G-8 ventured, "you should take me to the railroad station, *nicht wahr?* My appointment is for more than an hour hence, and at the station the restaurant will be open where I may eat my breakfast."

The car moved on two more blocks and drew up before the station. G-8 climbed out and bowed.

"*Danke schon, mein herren,*" he said and then closer, in a low whisper, "Remember, the *Vaterland* trusts you to forget me."

As heads bobbed, he was gone, trying to

keep back the smile that persisted in wrinkling his face.

He made sure that the two had driven away after his exit, then he made his way to the ticket window. A sleepy-looking old man yawned and stroked his moustache when asked the time of the next train for Freiburg. It was due to leave in less than an hour. G-8 bought a ticket and went into the little restaurant.

Later he boarded the train and settled into the cushioned seat of his compartment. The progress of the train was slow. There were many delays for freights that were taking provisions toward the front. It was late afternoon when G-8 stepped from the station at Freiburg. In the hours of daylight that remained, he walked to Ahornbaum Strasse and made a careful check of the house of *Herr Doktor* Frielinger and the community for several blocks about it.

The home of the electrical wizard was a humble dwelling of two stories and an attic. It was made of brick and set in an ample yard with a high hedge of lilac bushes that bordered both sides and the back. Across the front of the yard was a neatly-painted white picket fence.

Never once did G-8 walk on the same side of the street as the house that was number 32. When, early in the evening, he had the place with its surroundings well laid out in his mind, he went to a restaurant in the heart of town to eat and wait for darkness.

At ten minutes before nine, G-8 strolled leisurely along until he came to Ahornbaum Strasse. There he turned and walked along the side of the street where the house numbers were even. He passed number 20—the place where Augustine Hempel lived—and strolled on under the maple trees that gave the street its name.

Beyond, he came to the house of *Herr Doktor* Frielinger. He thought he saw a shadowy form move at the side of the house but he wasn't certain. There was only one way to learn whether the house was being watched by German police!

At the picket gate, G-8 paused, and adjusting his glasses, peered, as one whose sight was not clear, at the front door. Stealing a glance over his glasses, he could easily see the number 32 painted in white on a black background over the door, but he continued his scrutiny.

Hesitantly, he pushed the gate inward and began walking toward the front door. There was a dim light that glowed through the shade of one of the windows, but aside from that, the house was dark. The street lamp some hundred feet away brought out the number and the house details clearly.

Still squinting through the thick-lensed glasses, with head extended, G-8 made his way to the entrance. He didn't even turn when he heard a faint rustling on his left. That would be a guard coming to question and perhaps arrest him. The place was surely guarded.

G-8 was staring blindly at the doorway when a strong hand gripped his arm.

"Come away," a commanding voice hissed. "Come away without a sound and you will not be harmed. I must question you."

G-8 gave a perfect imitation of a scholarly man of fifty being startled.

"B-bitte," he stammered, "I—I do not understand. Or—" he smiled—"perhaps you have come to tell me what the number is. My eyes have failed me of late. I cannot see well, even with *mein* glasses. I am looking for number twenty."

While he talked, the guard was leading him across the lawn to a dark spot around the corner of the house. They stopped and G-8 had a moment to size up this guard. He was well-built, dressed in civilian clothes. In his right hand he gripped a Luger while he still held G-8 with the left.

"Now," the guard whispered in a husky, guttural, voice. "What are you doing here?"

"*Ach du Lieber,* I am not a thief," G-8 stammered. "Look at me. I do not look like a thief, do I, *mein herr?*" He raised his hand before his thick glasses. "*Mein* eyes, they are very poor. They say I am slowly going—*aber,* you are not interested in my troubles. I am looking for number twenty Ahornbaum Strasse."

"*Und* you mean to say," the guard demanded in the same low, rasping voice, "that you could not see those large numbers in the darkness?"

"*Bitte,*" G-8 answered. "I did not see the numbers. I could not find where they were."

G-8 knew instantly that the guard did not believe him. He hastened to allay his suspicion.

But the guard didn't seem to hear that last sentence. He ached up and laid hold of G-8's spectacles.

"I believe you are faking," he said. "If these glasses are not equipped with strong lenses, then you are under arrest."

He took the glasses from G-8's face, not very gently, and held them up toward the distant street light. For a long moment he stared through them while G-8 waited—knowing what the outcome would be.

"Here, *grossvater,* I do not see how anyone can look through lenses like that, anyway," he said. "But you have my pity."

The Master Spy groped for the glasses, then once they were in his hand, he laboriously slipped them on his nose and over his ears.

"*Und* what are you going to number 20 for?" the guard demanded.

"To see *mein* niece," G-8 said. He fumbled in his pockets for the clipping and brought it out. He made a pitiful gesture in trying to read it in the darkness and then he handed it to the guard.

"*Heir,*" he said, "*iss* a piece in the paper about Augustine, my niece, who led the patriotic parade of the children here in Freiburg over a week ago. I have taken time off to come and see her and bring her a little present for her noble work."

"Come," the guard nodded. "I'll show you number 20 and I'll read this when I get under a street light."

Several doors down the street, he stopped and glanced at the clipping. He nodded as he read the name and handed the clipping back to the Master Spy.

"It seems to be correct," he said. "Here is the house."

He turned G-8 and started him for the door. The Master Spy knew that the guard was waiting to see him enter, so he did not hesitate but thanked him and advanced boldly. Walking calmly up to the front door of Augustine Hempel's house, he knocked.

His brain was working fast as the footsteps within came nearer. The next procedure would depend largely upon who opened the door. The knob was turning and the door swung back.

A twelve-year-old girl stood in the doorway, peering out into the night at G-8. The Master Spy burst forth with a genial, disarming laugh.

"Hello Augustine," he cried. "*Und* how is the brave girl who leads the patriotic parades?"

With that, he stepped inside. The girl had smiled in answer to his laugh and his friendly greeting, but she backed away as he entered. He managed to close the door before she became suspicious. Suddenly fear flashed into her blue eyes. G-8 remembered there was a curtain on the door so that from outside, the guard couldn't watch them.

"*Mein* brave *fraulein*," the Master Spy whispered, bending down. "Do not cry out, for I have come as a friend. I have come to you because I know you are a brave girl. You must help your country by helping me."

He did not attempt to touch the girl but tried instead to win her confidence with his smile. Someone was coming from the rear room of the house. G-8 gave the girl a swift request.

"Please say that everything is all right," he begged.

The girl obediently lifted her voice and said an instant before the matron appeared in the hall doorway, "It's uncle, mother. Everything is all right."

The woman stared at G-8, her mouth open, but the Master Spy raised his finger to his lips in a sign for silence.

"*Bitte, Frau* Hempel," he requested, "I have just told your fine daughter, Augustine, that I need help. It is for His Majesty, the Kaiser. Even now, waiting outside, is a police officer in plain clothes to make sure that my reception here is welcome."

He turned to Augustine who was standing quite close to him.

"*Aber, mein fraulein*, why did you tell

114

your mother than I am your uncle? That was very fast thinking."

The girl was still a little frightened but she forced a smile.

"I thought that would keep mother still because, you see, I have an uncle who comes here to see us sometimes," she explained.

G-8 chuckled like a kindly old uncle might and said:

"That is excellent, because do you know what? I told the guard whom I left outside that I was your uncle. Isn't that funny?"

The girl admitted, laughing a little, that it was. The mother stayed her distance and demanded in a voice not unkind:

"*Bitte,* who are you and what do you want?"

"I," G-8 announced, proudly, "am special agent for His Majesty, the Kaiser. I have been sent here to secretly investigate the disappearance of *Herr Doktor* Frielinger. You knew him?"

The mother's eyes popped open.

"*Ach du Lieber!*" she breathed, half to herself. "Special agent for His Majesty." And then, as though she suddenly realized that a question had been asked of her, she colored with embarrassment and added hastily, "*Jawohl, mein herr. Herr Doktor und Frau* Frielinger have been very fine neighbors. It is horrible what has happened."

"*Jawohl*," G-8 nodded. "*Und* that is why I am here. There is a guard of supposed police officers about her house. Do you know about that?"

"Only," *Frau* Hempel admitted, "as I have seen them about now and then. Of course, I wondered. The neighbors say that they are trying to catch someone coming into the house."

"You mean, then," G-8 probed, "that rumor has it that perhaps spies from the enemy side of the lines have abducted the doctor in order to use his great extinguishing beam for themselves?"

The woman's face went white. "I do not know," she confessed. "Perhaps that is correct. I have been so worried, even of Augustine, when she goes out. If her father were only back from the war, I would feel much safer," she sighed. "But that cannot be."

"But I am not afraid, mother," the girl said stoutly.

"*Ja*, I know, Augustine," the mother nodded, patting the girl's shoulder. She turned to the Master Spy. "That is another thing which worries me," she admitted. "Augustine has no fear of anything."

"She is a very brave girl, I know," G-8 agreed. "But now that I am here, I hope I can count on your help, *Frau* Hempel?"

The woman did not hesitate in her answer.

"Anything for His Majesty, the Kaiser," she said. "What do you want?"

"Something very simple," G-8 told her. "I only require to be let out of your back door—quietly—and then it is the wish of His Majesty, the Kaiser, that I move in the greatest secrecy. Do you understand?"

G-8 let his eyes flash from the mother and rest upon the daughter's face. Both heads nodded and the faces were grave.

"It must be wonderful to be a secret operator," the girl breathed.

G-8 smiled now.

"It is very dangerous," he confessed. "I've been very lucky, Augustine. *Und* I am so glad that you live close to the house which I must enter. You have been a great help to me—*und* our Kaiser. I must talk with *Frau* Frielinger without the knowledge of the guards."

He turned toward the rear of the house.

Frau Hempel led the way to the back door. There was no light in that back room.

117

G-8 was at the door, waiting while *Frau* Hempel drew back the bolt. She opened it without a sound and G-8, with a farewell pat on the girl's shoulder, slipped out into the dark rear yard.

CHAPTER NINE
Man of the Night

No light had streamed out of the rear door. So far as G-8 could tell, he was alone in the night. He turned to the left, following the side of the house, and crouched there for some time to make sure that no one else was about.

Minutes passed. He heard the padding of feet inside and knew that *Frau* Hempel and her daughter had gone to the front of the house and were acting as though nothing had happened. They would keep their promise to the Master Spy and, as they thought, to their Kaiser.

When he was certain that he was not being watched, he crept silently to the rear boundary of the yard. There were two fruit trees that shadowed the space and helped him with their added shadow.

At the rear of the yard a four-foot wood fence blocked him. He skirted this, climbed over a wire entanglement, and was in the next yard. He climbed over now into the yard of a house facing on the next street, then on over a variety of fences and hedges.

He knew when he had come to the yard of *Herr Doktor* Frielinger, for the lilac hedge was higher than any of the other divisional structures and there was, too, the smell of lilacs that were just breaking into bloom.

Here his keenest cunning must be brought into play. He must outguess the guard who, he was certain, lurked somewhere along this back hedge. It seemed strange that a hedge of sweet smelling, beautiful flowers should shelter anything so sinister as a dog of war. He remembered a lilac bush at the corner of his home in the States when he was younger.

Up to now he had been moving in a crouched position, noiselessly. He changed his method. Straightening, he let some of the lilac bushes scrape by his clothing. A fragrant bunch of blossoms caressed his face. There was a rustling sound.

Now he heard what he expected. There

119

was an answering rustle in the hedge about fifteen feet ahead of him. Instantly, G-8 hissed across that space in a stage whisper.

"Is that you?"

It was a silly question when he didn't know who the other was, but it served his purpose. It would, he hoped, be assuring to the guard that he, G-8, felt that he was expected. At least he wasn't trying to disguise his movements.

And strangely enough, the answer came back, *"Jawohl,"* in a tense, almost inaudible whisper. "What is it?"

G-8 was moving toward the man in the hedge. He stretched out his hand and, touching the fellow's shoulder, crouched beside him.

"I have come from headquarters to relieve you," G-8 said. "The chief has sent me to take your place. There is something he wishes you to do."

He tensed for the answer which wasn't long in coming.

"The chief?" inquired the man. He was standing beside G-8 now—a man half a head taller than the Master Spy and much heavier. "I am the chief! What are you talking about?"

That was enough to stop an ordinary spy, but G-8 was thinking like mad.

"Eine minute, bitte," he whispered. "I will show you. I have written special orders from your superior and mine. Here."

He held out the identification papers that Nippy had forged for him before leaving Le Bourget. If this big guard could see them, they would not be very convincing, but it was dark.

"Ach!" G-8 hissed, *"bitte,* I forgot it is dark! Perhaps I can find *mein* light. Here, I have it sir. I will shine it for only a moment so that we are not seen. If you will, *mein herr,* keep your eyes on the paper and be ready for the light. *Das ist gut.* Now!"

G-8 hadn't picked his light from his pocket. Instead, he had lifted an ugly Mauser pistol, hammer fashion, and was raising it to strike. He saw the Hun bend his head down ready to read the special orders.

The pistol wasn't very heavy, so he had to put plenty of force in the blow. He was standing so that his right arm could swing freely and that was a help. He brought the pistol down with all possible force.

The guard never suspected his move until he had struck. There was the thud like the dropping of a cracked cocoanut and the body slumped. G-8 leaped in to catch it so that it wouldn't fall into the hedge with a crashing sound and alarm the other guards.

Gently he lowered it to the ground just outside the bushes, took a Luger from the pocket, reclaimed his identification papers, and stepped across through the hedge.

There in the shadows he waited for warning sounds. And while he waited, he made a study of his approach to the house. Like all of those back yards that he had passed through, there were fruit trees here that added to the gloom.

The back door, even though his eyes were very accustomed to the darkness now, was only a dark outline. He chose that as his point of entrance.

The rear door of *Frau* Hempel's house had been locked by a bolt at the back. He'd have some trouble with that, but the conventional type of key lock—his hand closed tentatively over a slim bundle of skeleton keys that were snugly wrapped in a soft leather case to guard against their making noise.

G-8 moved those keys from a secret pocket in his trousers to an outside pocket of his coat where they could be gotten at easily.

His crossing of the yard was slow. Nearly

ten minutes passed before he was standing in the rear doorway's shadow. The keys came out of his pocket and he tried the first without success. The second was no better than the first, but the third one turned easily. He heard a slight grating of the lock as it slid back.

Ever so slowly he pushed in the door. It was free except for the latch so he turned the knob and it opened. He dared open it only a fraction of an inch at a time to guard against squeaking. Slowly, he swung it back a little more than a foot. That was enough.

The Master Spy slipped through and closed it as silently from within, locking it again.

He caught a glow of light from the front room which showed him that he was in a sort of rear hallway. There was a door to the left that was partly open.

He moved into that room—a kitchen—and tiptoed on toward the room in front. Peering through the door, he saw a bed on which a small figure lay. There was something on the pillow turned toward him, but although there was hair at the top, there seemed to be no face. A closer look showed him that the head was small—

about the size of a boy of ten years—and, except for the hair, swathed in bandages.

On the other side of the room, sitting motionless in a chair beside the very dim table lamp, was a woman. She would be *Frau* Frielinger. There was a strip of white adhesive tape over her nose as though that member had been broken.

The woman sat pitifully with hands folded in her lap and eyes staring straight ahead. There was some neglected sewing in her lap.

The interior of the house was deathly still, so much so that G-8 wondered why the woman didn't hear his slight breathing. He could hear her across the room and once the boy roused a little to groan in his sleep.

When that happened, the mother's face twitched into an expression of pain and she jerked up quickly and shifted her eyes to the restless form of her son.

"Ach, Gott! Mein liebchen! Mein klein liebchen!"

But the boy slept on and the mother sighed, shuddered and then stared suddenly into the dark doorway where G-8 was standing. At the same instant, G-8 stepped into the light with a warning forefinger laid across his lips. He smiled and bowed.

"*Bitte, Frau Frielinger,* I am a friend," he announced. "Do not cry out. I have come to help you and your husband."

The woman looked as though she were going suddenly insane. Her eyes widened in a mad stare—her hands flew to her throat and she opened her mouth to scream.

G-8 could have rushed her and might have succeeded in clapping a hand over her mouth before she could cry out, but he took a long chance and bet on another method that would not antagonize her. Hurriedly, he said:

"Your son, *Frau* Frielinger, I am here to help him."

That seemed to snap her mind back to imperative things. She had half risen out of her chair when G-8 first spoke. Now she sank back with a resigned sigh.

"It does not matter," she choked. "Little more can happen to us. Who are you? What do you want?"

G-8 bowed low before her chair.

"*Bitte, Frau* Frielinger," he said, "I have come, as I told you, to help you and your husband and your poor little son there. If you will tell me what I wish to know, I will do my best to bring your husband back and bring the guilty one, *Herr Stahl-maske,* to punishment."

The woman shrugged and shook her head.

"You do not know what you are saying," she said. "How did you get in here?"

"May I answer that after I have asked you a few questions?" the Master Spy said. "Do you know who the men are that guard your house?"

The woman nodded without a change of expression.

"They are police officers sent by the government and dressed in plain clothes to spy upon those who come and go. I am not allowed out of the house. The grocer brings food and I wait. That is all."

"But why," G-8 demanded, "do they hold you under suspicion?"

"Because," *Frau* Frielinger said bitterly, "my husband believed in peace. He refused to use his inventions to kill the enemy. He said that he would not sleep at night if he knew that his wireless beam had disintegrated men. He had intended it for medical uses—for healing. The government thinks perhaps he had conspired against the *Vaterland.* You are from the government and do not believe me. You are here to trick me."

The woman had raised her voice to a dangerously high pitch. G-8 raised his finger in warning once more.

"*Bitte, Frau* Frielinger," he begged. "Not so loud—or those outside will know that you are talking to someone. I have decided to tell you truthfully who I am. You must believe me. I am not German, or for the German cause. I know very well that your husband, *Herr Doktor* Frielinger, has not turned over any invention to the Allies."

Frau Frielinger sighed and shook her head.

"If I could only be sure that you are here to help me," she breathed. "But that is impossible. Everyone is against us in our trouble. If *mein* husband had been perhaps a tailor or a meat cutter we could be happy without suspicion."

"It is not impossible," G-8 hastened to assure her. "Listen closely to me, *Frau* Frielinger."

He put his lips near to her ear and whispered, "I am G-8, the American spy!"

The woman's face went white.

"You!" she gasped. "You are really here to help me—to bring back my husband?"

"*Jawohl*," G-8 nodded. "If *Herr Stahl-maske* succeeds in the use of the extinguishing beam, he can wipe out our troops in a few hours. I must reach him in time to prevent his learning the secret from your husband."

Frau Frielinger rose from her chair and clutched the Master Spy's arm.

"Mein Herr," she said, "I must be certain. It is treason for me to help you, but my own people are against me. I want *mein* husband back. I have suffered enough."

"If you will help me," G-8 said, "I will give you my word. I will do all I can to help you and your husband, *Frau* Frielinger. The police are confused. They do not understand."

"Yes," she said, calm again, "I would rather think that. But I have decided! Come to the desk here."

She led G-8 to a large desk at the other end of the room. Lowering the front, she opened a panel and took out a small, flat box. It measured about six inches by four inches by one inch thick.

"This," she said, "is a pocket wireless set that my husband invented some months ago. He refused to let it be used in the war."

"And why do you show it to me?" G-8 asked.

"It is the only means of finding him," *Frau* Frielinger explained. "It is tuned to his set. I would have given it to the police but they would believe nothing I told them. Here, I will show you."

To G-8's astonishment, she snapped open the lid of the box and took out a small, cone-shaped object made of hard rubber. To the large end was attached a pair of wires and they vanished in the intricate workings of the box.

"This," she explained, "is the earphone. You place it in your ear and give it a slight turn so it will stay."

Frau Frielinger demonstrated on her own ear. There was also a tiny wireless at the other end of the box. There was a thin metal case over the working parts, leaving nothing but a two-way switch showing.

"Mein herr," she said in a hushed whisper. "I have received messages from *mein* husband every night at midnight. He tells me that he is still alive but"—her voice broke—"he cannot hold out much longer."

"Does he tell you where he is?" G-8 asked tensely.

She shook her head. "He does not know. He says it is a long, rough journey from Freiburg. He believes he is up several stairs, but he has not been able to see about him. He is blind, *mein herr*."

"That is terrible," G-8 sympathized. "You say he has a pocket radio set like this one?"

"Jawohl," the woman nodded. "It is smaller and the concentrated battery is becoming weaker. He only talks to me for a few minutes each night at midnight. He tells me that *Herr Stahlmaske* is afraid he will die before he gives him the secret, so he only tortures him during the day."

"Stahlmaske must be a considerate devil," G-8 ventured. *"Und* you can let me have this set to take with me, *Frau* Frielinger?"

Frau Frielinger nodded quickly and took the tiny ear phone from her ear. She replaced it in the case and held it out to G-8.

"You see, *mein herr,*" she explained, "if you wish to send a message, you push the switch over to the right, and if you wish to receive his message, you turn it to the left. It is in the center now—turned off completely."

G-8 nodded, closed the lid, and slipped the box into his inside coat pocket.

"Und now tell me about the beam," he asked. "You say it is really deadly, *Frau* Frielinger?"

The woman's face paled and she nodded.

"Mein herr," she said in an awed voice, "it is the most deadly instrument ever invented. The *doktor* worried night and day after he made his discovery for fear someone unscrupulous would gain control of it. He had only made one demonstration with it. Then the rat he turned it on *und* the table top *und* a portion of the side wall of the house disintegrated, leaving nothing but dust."

"You saw this, *Frau* Frielinger?" G-8 asked.

The woman nodded solemnly.

"With these two eyes," she said.

G-8 looked at his watch.

"It is growing late, *Frau* Frielinger," he said. "I must hurry if I am to be in the air by midnight."

"In the air?" the woman gasped. "*Aber,* I thought you were going to talk to him tonight—over the wireless."

"I am," G-8 nodded. "I've got to be flying so that I can get his direction. I'm satisfied that he is somewhere in the Black Forest. It will tell me whether I'm flying in the right direction or not. You see, the signals will grow dimmer as I go away from him and stronger if I am getting nearer."

The Master Spy bowed politely.

"*Und* now I must slip out of your back door and trust that I have as much luck eluding discovery as when I entered."

She walked with him to the back door and waited until he had slipped into the shadows. There he dropped on his stomach and began to crawl back along the row of low bushes.

He reached the lilac hedge and slowly got to his feet. Suddenly, he became a shadow-covered statue. There was a sound from close by. It was only the crackling of a very small twig and the light brushing of a few leaves, but it told him that someone was there within three feet of him. Someone—waiting!

CHAPTER TEN
Wings of Disaster

Two things happened simultaneously. The Master Spy flashed out a name that should bring the proper results, but in doing so, he was almost a split second too late to make it seem convincing.

As soon as he heard the sound and knew that someone was close to the body of the police chief, G-8 hissed in a clear whisper:

"*Herr anfuhrer*—Chief!"

At the same instant, something hard was poked into his side and he knew it was the muzzle of a gun.

He took a long chance and burst out with a low chuckle but he was careful not to move his body.

"*Ach, du Lieber, herr anfuhrer!*" he laughed, "That is a good joke on you. I come from the special mission into the house that you have sent me on and when I come back you suspect me as someone else and stick a gun into my—"

He got no farther, for the gun was prodded harder into his ribs and a guttural voice rasped out of the darkness.

"Silence! *Der anfuhrer* is dead."

"Dead!" G-8 breathed in astonished awe. "*Gott im Himmel!*"

"*Und* perhaps you are the one who knows most about his death, *Ja?*" the other snapped.

G-8 had tried to catch a familiar note in his voice. If it was the guard who had directed him to Augustine Hempel's house, then the sooner he got rid of him, the better. But if it was another of the guards, he might have a chance of doing a smoother job.

"*Aber, der anfuhrer* cannot be dead." G-8 groaned. "It is impossible! I left him here not more than half an hour ago. I have come from Metz by special request. I am a secret agent, and my work is to obtain information which is desired by His Majesty, the Kaiser. Who could have done this?"

The gun didn't press into his side so hard now. G-8 took hope and boldly moved away from the gun, kneeling at the same time.

"Let me see him," he breathed. "Where is he? *Und bitte,* stop holding that gun against my ribs as though I were a burglar."

He was feeling over the body of the chief. Now in the almost total darkness, he made out the figure of another guard. There came the soft padding of feet and a voice which G-8 instantly recognized as belonging to that first guard, spoke.

"Was ist?"

The taller guard beside G-8 was about to speak. The Master Spy heard his quick intake of breath but beat him to the first word.

"Silence! Go back to your station," G-8

snapped with a ring of authority in his voice. *"Macht schnell!"*

"Jawohl," the first guard answered obediently and hurried away before the second one could interpose.

"Silence!" G-8 hissed again to the second. "Do you realize what this will mean? The death of your *anfuhrer* will mean that you will be brought before a firing squad for permitting such a thing to happen. We must have time to clear up the mystery so that you can produce the guilty party when the announcement is made. I will help you all I can."

"Gott im Himmel!" the guard breathed. "Do you mean to say they will suspect me of this?"

G-8 stood up and faced him toe to toe. He poked his fingers against the other's chest to make his words more emphatic.

"You know the tension there is over this affair. You know that we are not sure what has happened. We are not sure whose side *Herr Stahlmaske* is fighting on. I tell you, *mein herr,* I believe that one of his agents has killed your chief. We must investigate quickly, but first we must take away the body. There is a car here we may use for that purpose?"

"Jawohl," the guard admitted. "What shall we do, carry him to it?"

"Certainly, *dummkopf!*" G-8 snapped. "He cannot walk. Come—you take the shoulders and go first and I will take his feet. All together."

The body came up limp as a sack of potatoes. They carried it from the back of the house and staggered into the deep shadows of the side yard. G-8 heard the other guard grunt and groan under the weight.

Halfway to the street, the Master Spy stopped.

"This is very heavy," he admitted. "Let us rest a minute."

The other willingly let down his end. G-8 could see him quite plainly in a shaft of light that shone through the side yard from a street lamp. The Master Spy moved closer to him. His right hand was drawing the chief's Luger from his pocket, club fashion.

He was going to use the old, simple trick of diverting attention that he had used since boyhood.

The Master Spy had come around the body casually and now stood in the same dim light shaft as the other. Suddenly, he tensed and pointed to the back street where

136

the tree branches cast strange shadows as they shifted to and fro in the breeze.

"Look!" G-8 hissed. "What is that?"

The Hun fell into the trap. He spun around and looked the way G-8 was pointing—directly away from him.

The execution of that act was swift and sure. G-8 had planned well. His right hand rose and fell like a bolt of lightning in the night. The butt of the heavy Luger struck true and sank a little way into the skull. The guard's body fell across the form of his dead chief.

G-8 turned quickly and strode to the back street. About a hundred feet down the street he made out a car, parked under an exceptionally large spreading maple.

A smile grew on his face as he came closer to it. It was a large black vehicle with a step at the rear and seats along each side of the dark interior. He climbed into the front seat and tried the switch. The key was still there and the big car was ready to go.

G-8 stepped out once more and focused his eyes on the painted letters on the side. He read:

POLIZEIWAGEN
FREIBURG

"You can't beat that much for service," the Master Spy chuckled. "The police wagon of Freiburg. That ought to get me places in a hurry."

He started back for the driver's seat, then hesitated and looked back to where the two police officers lay. Quickly, he retraced his steps and returned a moment later with the badge and credentials of the police chief.

As the engine started, G-8 breathed encouragement to the patrol wagon.

"Come on, Black Maria, we're going to the airdrome faster than you've ever been driven before. This has got to look important."

There was a grinding of gears and the car shot into motion. He drove reasonably slow until he was out of town, then he bore down and the old, top-heavy bus roared and swayed as he went charging for the airdrome that lay on the flats below Freiburg.

Once he saw a pair of lights blink behind him when he took a turn, but they were far back and gave him no immediate alarm. As he drove on, he seemed to have lost them.

He glanced at his watch. It was now fifteen minutes before twelve o'clock. He must be in the air by midnight, ready to contact and take his direction from *Herr Doktor* Frielinger.

The country grew level. To the left G-8 could see dark, square blotches of light and shadow and large, squat buildings lining one edge of a field. Those would be hangars.

He raced his engine as he swung into the field. Guards stepped out in front of him, flashing their lights in his face. G-8 slowed but did not stop.

"I'm the chief of police of Freiburg!" he yelled. "I must have a plane at once."

He yelled it again as the airdrome came suddenly to life. An *offizier* leaped on the running board and stuck his head in for a closer look at G-8.

The Master Spy drew back his coat and displayed the polished metal police badge that gleamed in the glow from the dash light.

"Jawohl, herr anfuhrer," the *offizier* shouted above the roar of the engine. "Drive to the end hangar. There is, I believe, a two-seater plane warming already."

"Gut," G-8 replied. "We go at once."

The Master Spy's foot grew heavy on the accelerator again. Mechanics scurried before the onrushing police patrol. G-8 found the bell cord and set up a loud clanging that added to the confusion and excitement that he was purposely creating.

He jammed on the brakes and skidded to a stop at the far end of the field. There was a Hannoveraner two-seater with an Opal-Argus engine ticking over while mechanics checked.

"Macht schnell!" the *offizier* shouted to them. "Prepare the plane for instant flight."

The *offizier* had leaped from the running board of the car. G-8 was running close behind. He heard the nearest mechanic make an answer.

"Herr Leutnant," he saluted, "The plane is already to fly at once. We have just been making final checks. It is ordered ready at dawn."

"It will be back at dawn," the *leutnant* nodded. "Come, *herr anfuhrer,* we take off first, then you will find a speaking tube in the rear cockpit through which we can talk. When we are in the air, you will tell me where you wish to be taken."

Even as he spoke, he was climbing into the front cockpit. G-8 was in the rear seat.

With a roar, the one hundred and eighty horsepower Opal-Argus sent the whirling propeller kicking up a cloud of dust. The two-seater lumbered into motion. They droned across the dark field and climbed into the night.

G-8 found the speaking tube and spoke through it.

"Bitte, Herr Leutnant," he said, "I wish to be taken to an altitude of perhaps five thousand feet. Perhaps you will think this is strange. I am not so much interested in going anywhere as to make a test."

"A test, *mein herr?"* the *leutnant* ventured skeptically.

"Jawohl," G-8 answered. "But not with this plane. I will make the test with a certain wireless apparatus which I have. It must be sufficient to tell you that I have been in charge of secret work about the house of *Herr Doktor* Frielinger at Freiburg. You have read about him and his wonderful death invention, I suppose?"

"Jawohl," the *leutnant* answered, interested. "There was something about a story of a man with a steel mask who kidnaped him. He is suspected of being one of the Allies, perhaps working with the *verdammt* one, G-8, *nicht wahr?"*

"That is what we fear," G-8 said. "It is my work to discover where the *Herr Doktor* has been taken for there we will find the demon with the steel mask as well."

He glanced at his watch once more. It was one minute before midnight. He slipped the wireless case from his pocket, released the lid and inserted the earphone plug in his left ear. He pushed the switch to the receiving side, plugged his right ear with his finger to keep out engine noise and tensed to listen.

Seconds dragged by with maddening leisure. Then there came, ever so faintly, the humming of a code. G-8 strained to pick up the message that flashed to him so dimly. He spelled out the words. They were coming with astounding speed, but he was following.

I HAVE NOT BEEN ABLE TO TELL WHERE I AM. IT IS HIGH UP SOMEWHERE FOR I CAN HEAR TREE TOPS RUSTLE AND THE BIRDS SING IN THE MORNING. THE TORTURES I HAVE BEEN THROUGH THIS LAST DAY HAVE ALMOST FORCED ME TO GIVE UP THE SECRET BUT NOT QUITE. I CANNOT HOLD ON MUCH LONGER. PLEASE CAN YOU NOT GET HELP TO ME IN SOME WAY? I AM DESPERATE.

The Master Spy pushed the switch over to the sending side and began ticking the key rapidly. He was sending a reply to *Herr Doktor* Frielinger. A reply of encouragement and hope.

HERR DOKTOR FRIELINGER. I AM G-8 THE AMERICAN SPY. I HAVE JUST TALKED WITH YOUR WIFE AND AM NOW FLYING IN A GERMAN PLANE IN THE HOPE OF FINDING YOU. I AM COMING AS FAST AS I CAN. SEND ME OTHER MESSAGES EVERY FIVE MINUTES. I WILL FLY IN A STRAIGHT COURSE MEANTIME AND SEE IF YOUR SIGNALS AT THE END OF FIVE MINUTES ARE STRONGER OR WEAKER.

Again G-8 swung over the switch and listened to the answer.

I DO NOT KNOW WHY YOU ARE TRYING TO HELP ME BUT I WILL DO AS YOU SAY. IN FIVE MINUTES, AS NEARLY AS I CAN GUESS, I WILL SEND YOU ANOTHER MES-SAGE AND EACH FIVE MINUTES FROM THEN ON UNTIL YOU TELL

ME TO STOP. BUT THERE IS VERY LITTLE TIME LEFT. MY BATTERY IS NEARLY EXHAUSTED.

The Hun pilot turned about and stared back through the darkness at G-8. The Master Spy waved and spoke into the tube.

"The experiment is working perfectly," he assured the German. "Fly straight on the course as you are headed."

"*Jawhol,*" came the reply.

G-8 could see by the compass up front that the Hannoveraner was pointed slightly south of west. He guessed that was the wrong direction but he let the experiment take its course.

Five minutes passed. Meanwhile, he was tuned in because *Herr Doktor* Frielinger must guess at the time.

After almost exactly five minutes, the humming started again in the ear piece. It was very indistinct now. G-8 could scarcely catch the signals. He shouted to the pilot.

"Turn around quickly and fly east."

The pilot banked the two-seater about. The signals grew slightly stronger while they lasted. G-8 sent an answer.

YOU ARE TO THE EAST OF US.
I AM SURE NOW THAT YOU ARE
HELD SOMEWHERE IN THE BLACK
FOREST. WILL BE WAITING FOR
YOUR NEXT SIGNALS.

Minutes dragged on and the Hannoveraner droned to the east. Once more the pilot, driven by curiosity, turned in his seat and G-8 assured him through the tube that "everything was working nicely."

In four and a half minutes the signals came again. This time they were strong. G-8 caught them without any trouble at all.

SENDING MESSAGES AS OR-
DERED SO THAT YOU MAY CHECK
MY LOCATION.

That was repeated over and over again for two minutes. It grew louder all the time. Once more, the master spy sent back an answer.

REPEAT AGAIN IN FIVE MIN-
UTES. WE ARE GETTING CLOSER.

Four minutes passed and G-8 spoke to the pilot.

"You have flares?"

"*Jawohl.*"

"Be ready to drop one when I give you the signal. I must learn where we are."

"You are now over the Black Forest," the pilot told him. "Do you see that blotch of dots over there? That is the town of Waldheim."

"*Danke,*" G-8 answered.

Waldheim, then, was near La Rocque Castle, that half-ruined feudal fortress atop the rock cliffs that lifted above the rest of the country.

He called through the tube.

"*Herr leutnant,* do you know anything about the present use of La Rocque Castle?"

"So far as I know," the pilot told him, "it is not being used. There are enough stories of ghosts and haunts in the castle to keep anyone away from there. Besides, it is half in ruins."

"*Jawohl,*" G-8 agreed. But he was searching the Black Forest for it and he thought he saw it, pushing its cracked towers above the highest tree tops.

The signals began coming again after five minutes. They were very loud. G-8 shouted in the midst of them to his pilot.

"Drop a flare and head your plane straight for La Rocque Castle at once."

The flare plopped out. The nose of the Hannoveraner lowered and the plane picked up speed. The humming of the radio signals were ever growing stronger as they headed down the beam. But there was something in the message that caused G-8 to give another order quickly. *Herr Doktor* Frielinger was saying with his key:

I CAN HEAR THE DRONE OF A PLANE COMING NEARER. IF THAT IS YOUR SHIP I WOULD ADVISE GOING AWAY. YOU MUST AP-PROACH MORE STEALTHILY. *HERR STAHLMASKE* HAS THE BEAM MA-CHINE. HE CAN DESTROY YOU AND YOUR PLANE INSTANTLY. GET AWAY WHILE THERE IS TIME.

G-8 transferred that order to the *leutnant* and the big two-seater lumbered over and started away. Now that the Master Spy knew that *Herr Doktor* Frielinger was in the La Rocque Castle, there was no need of flying any closer.

As they sped away, he began to plan his movements. He could use the uniform on the pilot. He was about his size. There were dual controls in the rear cockpit. That part of it would be quite simple. He looked

147

back and saw the flare still drifting down on its parachute, flooding the Black Forest with light and picking out the castle on its promontory like a crumpled piece of quartz raised on an ebony setting.

The Master Spy felt about for a suitable weapon. But another circumstance came to save the life of the *leutnant* for the moment.

Lights suddenly began blinking from far to the southwest. G-8 watched them, fascinated by something familiar about their comings and goings.

After a few flashes, he recognized them as signal lights. They, too, were sending signals in dot-dash system. Why, that was in the secret code that only he and Nippy and Bull knew. They were sending the same words over and over again.

LA ROCQUE CASTLE. LA ROCQUE CASTLE.

Nippy and Bull were coming into the danger zone to tell him that *Stahlmaske* had his headquarters in La Rocque Castle, when he, G-8, had already found that out himself. But how had they learned of it?

"Mein herr," the *leutnant* cried. "Do

148

you see those flashing lights over there? They must come from other airplanes."

"Jawohl," G-8 answered. "Fly closer to them so that we can tell who they are and what they are doing here."

The big Hannoveraner turned quickly and headed for the light flashes. G-8 strained to see the fire darting from their exhaust stacks. The flash signals had stopped for the moment.

The sky ahead of them was black. He contemplated once more putting the *leutnant* out of the way, but that could wait until he had come into closer contact with Nippy and Bull.

The signals started up again, five minutes later.

LA ROCQUE CASTLE. LA ROCQUE CASTLE.

"Can you read their signal, *mein herr?"* the *leutnant* asked.

"Nein," G-8 lied. "A little closer."

Then something happened that took all other thoughts from G-8's mind. A strange power seized hold of him and his pilot and their ship. They couldn't get their breath. The *leutnant* was gasping, trying to speak, but without success.

G-8 was aware of several things. His middle felt as though a large amount of alum had been released there and was tending to draw all the rest of his body toward that nerve center. The engine of the Hannoveraner had stopped dead. They were falling in a sickly spin and the *leutnant* seemed able to do nothing about it.

CHAPTER ELEVEN
Stahlmaske Strikes

G-8 was fighting to get control of that whirling plane. The stick and rudder felt as though they were lashed fast. But his own muscles did not act freely to the will of his brain. Every part of his body was drawn taut—seemed tied up in knots.

In the reflected light from the flare they had dropped, the head of the *leutnant* in the front cockpit stood out. Perhaps the pilot's limp body would offer less resistance on the controls.

G-8 found it difficult even to draw the

Luger from his pocket and raise it to aim, but he managed it. The explosion of the gun seemed far away. His ear drums weren't functioning normally. Everything was contorted.

He had aimed at the base of the *leutnant's* skull. The head snapped forward due to the limpness of death and the force of the bullet. The controls of the plane were movable once more.

After a struggle he brought the Hannoveraner out of its deadly spin and upon an even keel. He stared about frantically for Nippy and Bull. The flare had gone out and darkness surrounded him. His eyes didn't act normally, for even they suffered from that tendency to be pulled inward.

Suddenly, the ghastly force vanished. G-8 was left breathless with the big two-seater going down in a long, gradual dive for the trees of the Black Forest.

He dropped a flare and when the magnesium lighted, stared in search of his Battle Aces. He found them gliding down toward a dull blotch of field that showed plainly in the ghostly white flare. It was easily within their gliding range.

As the Master Spy glided down, he raised from his seat, leaned forward and pulled the upper portion of the dead pilot's body partly out of the cockpit. He was going to need that uniform as free from blood as possible.

After a struggle and the loss of another thousand feet he managed to hang the body over the padded cowling of the front cockpit in such a way that the blood flowing from the wound in the head would run down the side of the fusilage and not down the collar of the coat and shirt.

The Master Spy took stock of other things below. Nippy and Bull had tried to revive their engines, but without luck. G-8's propeller was still turning over. He made a last minute try at it by clicking the switch back and forth and working the throttle. But the engine was truly dead, beyond aerial repair. The field that the Battle Aces had chosen lay in the center of a thinner tree growth. Obviously, at one time this had been a fair-sized farm, but in later years only the flatter portion had been worked, permitting the surrounding cleared land to grow up into bushes and scraggly, small weeds.

Nippy was already gliding into the field and Bull was close behind him. G-8 dropped one more flare and turned to come in. Now, for the first time, he caught sight of lights bobbing along on a road that led from the Black Forest toward the field.

A strong suspicion rose within him. *Stahlmaske* had sent the cars out to investigate these planes. G-8 had a plan worked out that might prevent capture. The big Hannoveraner jolted and rumbled to a stop. He leaped out to meet Nippy and Bull running toward him.

"Quick!" he shouted. "Help me get this pilot's body out."

He was straining at the form. Bull and Nippy made that simple. The Battle Aces stripped the uniform from the dead Hun pilot while G-8 took off his own uniform. Quickly he dressed in the other outfit, strapped the Luger holster to his side and jerked the gun out, holding it on Nippy and Bull and marching them toward the road as the cars drove up.

It was dark and the flash lights from those who piled from the autos somewhat blinded the Master Spy. The men from the cars, a dozen in all, were upon him before he could see them clearly.

That first glimpse of the faces was quite a shock. They were brutes of the ugliest possible description.

There was a big, hulking one in the lead whose head was almost flat in front and whose nose was four times the normal size. It made him look like an elephant with a clipped trunk. The eyes were tiny and wicked and set wide apart. The great mouth stretched nearly from ear to ear and was half hidden by the bulbous end of the oversized nose.

He sort of sniffed as he bellowed in German:

"You are under arrest!"

G-8 had meant to get the first word in, but he hadn't been sure of these brutes. Now he said:

"*Bitte,* they are my prisoners, *mein herr.* I shot them down myself and I am taking them to Waldheim to obtain verifications for my two victories."

The other laughed.

"Who do you think you are? You, a *leutnant,* telling me, *Herr Stahlmaske's* chief aide, what to do. Now I will tell you what goes on. You are coming with me, all three of you, to *Herr Stahlmaske.* He will decide who gets the credit for these captures. Come!"

He turned toward the waiting cars. G-8, Nippy, and Bull were pushed into the rear seat of the first car. The leader crowded behind the wheel and turned the car about.

The rest of the brutes followed in the other cars. Through the darkness the procession gained speed and soon they were winding through the steep roads of the Black Forest. Conversation with Nippy and Bull was too dangerous, for another brute, a squat fellow with a flat face on a head twice the normal size, had turned around in the front seat so that he could see the movements of G-8 and his Battle Aces.

It was later in the great banquet hall of La Rocque Castle that G-8 and Nippy and Bull first faced *Herr Stahlmaske.*

The brute towered at least two inches above Bull Martin. He stood in the center of the hall and about him in a half circle, his brute men leered at the procession of their fellows who brought with them as prizes, Nippy and Bull.

G-8 strode in behind them. Up until the moment when they had stopped in the rutted road that had once been the stone paved courtyard before the castle, he had clutched the Luger. But now it was gone. The brute leader had seen to that.

In these early hours of morning, electric lights hanging chain fashion about the back wall of the great chamber lent a strange atmosphere to the old and crumbling ruins.

Bats fluttered in corners, vainly searching for their world of darkness.

Herr Stahlmaske was dressed in a German uniform as were the others about him. They were a motley crew, unkept, ghastly-looking, and for the most part, filthy.

Stahlmaske waited until all had their places and the banquet hall was still as death. His eyes glowed like crimson brands through the slits in the steel, cone-shaped helmet mask that sat on his shoulders. The blazing eyes were not on Nippy or Bull, but upon G-8.

The Master Spy felt them fairly burning into his very soul. He struggled to keep perfect control of himself. He was the German flying *offizier* who had shot down and captured these two Americans!

He broke the silence with that announcement, finishing with:

"*Bitte*, I request that your men give my report the verification that it deserves. I landed immediately after disabling their engines."

Stahlmaske's huge shoulders moved as though he were laughing, and a hollow, hacking chuckle—inhuman and nerve-racking—came out of the hole in the mask where his mouth should be.

"Ach, das ist gut!" he croaked. "You tell me that you shot down these two *Amerikaners?"*

G-8 had known this was coming and he was ready.

"Bitte," he cut in, "I am quite sure that I shot them down. I made out their markings in the light of the flares that I dropped. Perhaps you could see those flares from here. I fired into the engines of both but, of course, in the dim light. I could not follow my shots into their cowlings. However, shortly after I fired, they came spiraling down to land at the field where your men found us. I went down at once and made them prisoners."

Stahlmaske hesitated for an instant. It was plain to G-8 that for a brief moment, he was not certain. He laughed again to cover his hesitation and then:

"Dummkopf!" he rasped hollowly. "I suppose you mean to tell me that you did not know that I turned on the extinguishing beam and stopped all of your motors in that way."

"Ach du Lieber!" G-8 gasped. "You mean to say that—"

He paused and let *Stahlmaske's* laugh cut him off. But *Stahlmaske* was laughing at something far more sinister than G-8 guessed. The Master Spy was taken completely off guard when *Stahlmaske* bellowed:

"I have played with you long enough, *verdamnt* one. You thought I was about to believe the story of your being a German *leutnant*. You thought you were making a fool of me like you have made of *Herr Doktor* Kreuger and others!"

The brute laughed in high triumph.

"Gott im Himmel, this is my moment!" he said. "I have here the man who shot me from the balloon basket and made me like I am—so horrible that the world would shudder to look upon what is left of my face. You think that you have tricked me, but you are for once mistaken, *verdammt* one. I know you are G-8!"

The vaulted halls screamed with the echo of mad laughter until skulking rats dived for their holes and bats battered their heads blindly against the stones in their frantic efforts to get away from the ghastly sound.

The Master Spy stood motionless. Nippy shot a questioning glance at him as if to say, "Where do we go from here, chief?" Bull shifted nervously, like a pent-up fighting machine eager to spring into action.

And in the faces of the brutes and *Herr Stahlmaske,* G-8, Master Spy that he was, shook with mirth and chuckled, as though the giant fiend in the mask had just finished telling about a humorous incident.

The laughter from *Stahlmaske* and the others suddenly ceased and except for G-8's laughter, which rippled on for a moment, the banquet hall was still. Brutes, now in an ugly mood, moved closer to their demon leader in anticipation of sudden action.

The chuckle died and G-8 spoke.

"Herr Stahlmaske," he bowed, "may I be the first to offer my congratulations. You've made rather a clean sweep of your enemies. Permit me"—he turned toward Bull—"to present my assistants, Bull Martin and"—he turned and swept a graceful arm toward the terrier ace—"Nippy Weston."

"Donnerwetter!" Stahlmaske blasted. "*Und* perhaps you are going to try and convince me that you will work on my side. Save your breath, *dummkopf.* We need no help from you."

"For once in your life," G-8 replied, still smiling and keeping his voice to a normal pitch, "you are wrong, *Herr Stahlmaske.* My introduction of my assistants was done, you might say, in the form of a confession. There is nothing more we may hope for. I assume that we, and particularly I, will be used for experimental purposes with your disintegrating wireless beam. *Frau* Frielinger had told me what a horrible death it will be."

"*Frau* Frielinger?" *Stahlmaske* croaked. "She has told you about the beam?"

G-8 smiled and nodded at leisure.

"To be sure," he answered. "I had a very pleasant visit with her in her home. You knew, of course, that I have been there, but you did not know that she told me secrets of the beam that even you have not yet learned. I have written them down and have sent them to the Allied side of the lines. They are working now on a device such as you have, but we can make many. You have only the original."

"You lie!" *Stahlmaske* thundered, beside himself with uncertainty. "You lie, otherwise, you would not tell me this."

G-8 shrugged calmly.

"Again you are wrong, *Herr Stahlmaske*. You see, I have simply explained that I know how horrible a death this disintegrating will be. So—" he shrugged again— "I wish to get it over with as quick as possible."

He shot a glance at *Stahlmaske* and took another desperate step in his hurried plan. Turning to Nippy and Bull, he asked:

"You agree with me, gentlemen? You

also wish to die at once by the beam, rather than wait?"

Nippy and Bull nodded obediently. But there was much in the looks that each gave the Master Spy, showing that they thought him suddenly insane.

"That's settled, then," G-8 nodded. "You see, the greatest horror in our lives, *Herr Stahlmaske,* has been waiting—not knowing what moment we should die. Usually, there is no prolonged pain in death. We three suffer mental pain to a much greater degree than others for the simple reason that we use our mental powers much more than most people. So may I beg of you, *Herr Stahlmaske,* for myself and my assistants, kill us with the ray now, and end this horrible uncertainty."

The brutes had moved in so that they formed a close ring about the three prisoners. *Stahlmaske* had not moved from the one spot during G-8's entire speech. His whole body was shaking with indecision. Suddenly, he burst out in a bellow roar of rage.

"Take them to the dungeon room!" he cried. "Three of you guard the entrance. I will have my revenge. I will deal with them at an unannounced time—not far away."

His red eyes blazed and he continued.

"You will suffer the torments of mental hell. *Und* when I decide to turn on the beam, I shall make it as slow and painful as possible. I shall get rid of you slowly, an arm or leg at a time."

Nippy took the cue. He rushed forward with outstretched, supplicating hands.

"Bitte, Herr Stahlmaske," he pleaded. "Be merciful! Kill us now and let us rest in peace."

Brutes snatched the terrier ace back and dragged him toward the far end of the great hall. Others dragged G-8 and Bull, who was making an excellent show of his resistance.

Pulling, tearing and cursing them, the brutes dragged their prisoners down the stone stairs to the under part of the old castle. Stones were loose beneath their feet. A heavy door swung open in the dimly-lighted labyrinth of corridors. They were plunged into a dark hole and the great door clanged shut behind them.

For the first minute, the three took time to get their balance and orient themselves. There was a wide grating in the door through which the dim light streamed. In a few moments, the eyes of the three became accustomed enough to the darkness to enable them to see each other and their surroundings.

Bull was first to speak.

"Holy Herring!" he blurted. "I never was so sure that anybody was nuts as I was of you."

"Shhhhh," G-8 warned in a whisper. "Remember there are three guards outside our door."

"Okay," Nippy hissed, "but I felt the same way Bull did. Boy, you had my hair standing on end, G-8! I thought sure you'd given up and wanted to get it over as soon as you could."

"I still think it was more luck than anything else," Bull ventured, "that made *Stahlmaske* decide to wait."

"When you win in a deal like that," G-8 smiled, "you can always rack most of it up to luck, getting the breaks, or whatever you may call it. Anyway, we've got a little time to work. To tell you the truth, I was desperate. Before I spoke, I expected *Stahlmaske* to bring out his gadget and start work on us right there in the hall. I'm glad we bluffed him."

"That would sure be a funny sensation," Nippy grinned. "He'd get out his magic lantern or vanishing machine or whatever he calls it. You turn around and shake hands with me to say good-by and then all of a sudden I'm gone. I'll bet you'd feel foolish shaking hands with nothing. Talk about looking sheepish."

"Holy Herring, squirt!" Bull groaned. "This isn't any time to make wisecracks. Do you know that any minute we're liable to go up in smoke?" He turned to G-8. "Or is this guy with the closed-in stove pipe on his head just kidding us?"

"He's not kidding," G-8 assured. "You felt the action of the beam when you were flying a little while ago. We must have been ten miles away from here. If the beam is that powerful at ten miles, it ought to be pretty potent at fifty or a hundred feet."

"You think it really does make you vanish—sort of disintegrate you, so that there's nothing much left?" Bull asked.

"Absolutely," G-8 nodded. "But let's go back an hour or so. How is it that you two came highballing over to tell me that *Stahlmaske* was in La Rocque Castle?"

"We thought you would want to know, and we figured you'd be somewhere in this general location. You said you suspected *Stahlmaske* was in the vicinity of Freiburg," Nippy told him.

"Sure," G-8 nodded patiently. "But how

164

did you find out that it was La Rocque Castle?"

"Remember the leader of the ugly-looking foursome that came to get you at the hangar?" Nippy asked. "Well, he confessed, to keep himself from being shot. He told us where *Stahlmaske's* quarters were."

Bull was pacing the great, dank stones of the dungeon floor restlessly.

"What I want to know," he grumbled, "is how we're going to get out of here. I'll be nuts in another ten minutes, waiting for that beam to be turned on. I'm expecting to lose a leg or an arm any minute."

"You could lose about half of that carcass of yours, you big ox," Nippy grinned, "and still have a lot left."

"All right, squirt," Bull shot back. "But for once in my life, I'd like to shrink up and slide through the grating in that door and get moving."

There was a sudden pause, broken by Nippy.

"Hey, listen," he said, "I have an idea. If this works, we'll be out of here and moving plenty in less than ten minutes." He turned to the Master Spy and asked, "Have you got your make-up kit, G-8?"

"As usual," the Master Spy admitted.

"All right," Nippy hurried on. "Listen.

You've got a little bottle of ammonia in that kit, haven't you?"

"Yes," G-8 admitted, "I use it for mixing one of Battle's ingredients, but what's the idea of—"

"Listen," Nippy cut in. "Take out your case and give me that little bottle, will you? Now here's what we'll do."

G-8 handed over the bottle of ammonia and Nippy raced on:

"We'll blow this ammonia into the eyes of the guards and that will make them—"

"Hey, wait a minute," Bull growled. "How are we going to blow ammonia or anything else into the eyes of the guards if we haven't got anything to blow it through? Maybe you want us to throw them ammonia kisses."

"Yeah," Nippy admitted. "That's right. I forgot. I sort of figured we could just go to the drug store and get some soda straws and—"

"Or some bean shooters," Bull cut in.

"Hey, wait," the terrier ace hissed. "What's this around our feet?"

A rustling sound came to their ears as he kicked about toward one corner of the dungeon.

"Straw," he gasped, bending down. "It's

old, but maybe it will do. All we've got to do is find three pieces big enough and straight enough to make bean or ammonia shooters."

There was a gentle scramble along the floor at the end of which the three rose triumphant.

"We're all set," Nippy breathed excitedly. "We each have a straw, so we pour it full of ammonia and hold the bottom end to keep it from running out. We'll call over the guards, get them close to the grating of the door and then when I say blow, we let them have it right in the eyes. We line up and pick the guy that's opposite us. Get it?"

"Right," G-8 nodded. "So what?"

"When they get the ammonia in their eyes, they'll start running. They won't think about anything but their eyes."

"If you ask me," Bull grunted, "it sounds crazy. We got them running down the corridor, but we're still locked up here in the dungeon. They aren't keeping us in here, it's the lock on the outside of the door, and we can't reach it from inside. I looked."

"Sure," Nippy admitted. "But when they run, you, G-8, holler in perfect German, 'They've escaped. G-8 and his assistants

167

are getting away', and we'll see what happens. From then on you do as I say. All set?"

"It still sounds dumb to me," Bull admitted, "but anything is better than standing here, waiting until that guy does the vanishing act on us. When do we start?"

"Right now," Nippy told him. "Come on over to the door."

They followed the terrier ace to the door. Each one held his straw filled with ammonia by pinching the lower end. They lined up in front of the door. The three guards were plainly visible outside. One turned around and stared at the slit.

"Hey, you three!" Nippy cracked. "Let us out of here! Come on, you ugly-looking mutts—get close enough and I'll smack your homely faces."

The three brutes turned and glared. They brought up their guns in a threatening attitude. G-8 and his Battle Aces raised their straws in preparation.

"Blow!" Nippy ordered.

CHAPTER TWELVE
Aces Wild!

At the signal from Nippy, all three raised their straws. Each man picked his opponent through the bars and pointed his straw straight for his eyes. There was a quick intake of breath and then the sound of liquid spraying through the air.

As though at a given signal, the three ugly brutes clapped their hands to their eyes as the ammonia blinded them. One cried out with pain and the other two turned and started running blindly down the corridor. The sound of their feet pounding the great stones of the floor echoed from the vaulted, crumbled walls.

At that moment, G-8 bellowed in a disguised, gutteral voice, "Stop them! G-8 and his assistants are escaping!"

He yelled it again and again through the bars. Then Nippy pulled him back from the door. Others were shouting by now.

In a fast whisper, Nippy was giving orders:

"Now here's the way it's going to work from now on," he said. "Some of these smaller stones that make up the floor are loose. Pick some up in your hands. I think *Stahlmaske* will suspect something funny and before he does anything else, he'll come down here and look in. But he won't see us because we'll be hiding right under his nose, down here by the door where it's dark. He'll unlock the door and come in to make sure that we've gone, while the rest of his men chase those three with the ammonia in their eyes. He may not be alone, but at any rate, we'll make a break for it. Bull, you lead the way. You'll probably have some line-bucking to do and these brutes aren't going to be any tin soldiers to bowl over."

"O. K.," G-8 agreed. "We're all set. Quiet! I think *Stahlmaske* is coming now on the run."

They could hear the sodden beat of heavy boots outside the door. Someone was looking inside the grill, breathing heavily. An angry curse sounded and then:

"I cannot see them in here. Wait; I will unlock the door to make sure."

They heard the heavy bolt sliding back

and the door was thrown open. *Stahlmaske* himself barged in, followed by three of his ugly henchmen.

"Let's go," G-8 hissed.

The Master Spy and his Battle Aces sprang from their hiding places behind the door. The paving stones came up and connected with the heads of the brutes. Two of them went down; *Stahlmaske* and the third turned to fight.

Bull Martin rushed the giant fiend with head down and his right shoulder and fist forward. He struck him in the pit of the stomach with the force of a battering ran. *Stahlmaske* grunted as the air went out of his big chest. He was borne over backward. Bull struck again, but by now, Nippy had lashed in from the side. As G-8 let a right fly to the jaw of the one remaining brute, he saw Nippy grab the steel helmet mask that the fiend wore and jerk it around in a half turn. Then the terrier ace pushed Bull away.

"Come on!" he yelled. "We've got to get out of here while there's still time. I got Goliath's stove-pipe turned around so he don't know whether he's coming or going."

Other booted feet were approaching— more brutes to help in the chase. G-8 whirled and charged through the door with

Nippy and Bull close behind him. They were cut off from the stairs, down which they had been dragged, by more than a dozen men who were coming from that direction. G-8 and his Battle Aces swerved and raced down the corridor in the opposite direction. Four hulking brutes were approaching from that direction.

"Follow your interference!" Bull yelled, charging forward with lowered head.

The men blocked the passage and braced themselves for the attack. G-8's hand was on Bull's back and Nippy was running in the same position as the Master Spy. They were braced to push each other through that line. Beyond was a partly opened door.

The human battering ram struck that wall of scarred flesh and *Stahlmaske's* men flew against the sides of the corridor. Before they could regain their balance, Nippy and Bull, and G-8 had charged through and were making for the door. The door flew open before Bull's onslaught and he plunged headlong out into the darkness with G-8 and Nippy streaking behind him.

For a brief instant, they dropped into space, then they were scrambling wildly and splashing about. Cold water penetrated their clothing.

"We'll get you, you big ox," Nippy chirped.

"You lead us out of the cooler into an ice pond."

"Nuts," Bull spluttered. "How did I know this was the moat that surrounded the castle?"

"Not so loud," G-8 hissed. "Swim for the other side as fast as you can. They're after us now."

The sound of running feet came to their ears and all three struck out for the opposite side of the great ditch. They reached the bank and began scrambling up the ancient stone wall of the moat. They had just reached the underbrush when a flashlight beam stabbed out over the water and focussed full on them. But it was only for an instant. G-8 ducked behind a bush and dropped flat. A gun cracked and the bullet cut a twig above his head and whistled off through the trees.

The Master Spy led his Battle Aces along the edge of the moat through the thick brush. It would be logical, he knew, for *Stahlmaske* and his brutes to expect them to climb directly up the low bank of the moat in order to get out of range as quickly as possible. The attackers continued to fire into the brush over the spot where the three had first climbed out of the water.

Meantime, G-8 and his Battle Aces climbed over the ridge farther down where it was dark. Once free, they ran out around to the front of the great chateau. Three cars were waiting there. Stealthily, G-8 and his Battle Aces crept up on those cars. No one seemed to be about; all attention at the time had been concentrated on the capture of the three in the dungeon corridors. The Master Spy halted behind a screen of brush, drew the tiny wireless set from his boot, and handed it to Bull.

"Take care of this," he ordered, "and be listening for me. I may want to send you a message if I contact *Herr Doktor* Frielinger." He turned to the terrier ace. "Nippy, you get in this last car," he said. "Bull, you and I are going to disable these other two busses so that they won't be able to follow us."

The three strode across the opening to the parked cars. Nippy slid in behind the wheel of the last car in the line.

"Start the engine," G-8 ordered, "and back the car around so we will be ready to go."

Bull was working on the first car in the row and G-8 was giving his attention to the center one when Nippy started the engine. Quickly, the Master Spy raised the hood of his car, grasped a handful of wires and pulled hard. The wires came loose and he threw them into the brush nearby.

Nippy was backing the car around. There was wild shouting from the interior of the castle. Men were running toward the front door as G-8 and Bull leaped aboard Nippy's car. Nippy sent the car tearing down the road that led along the face of La Rocque cliff.

"You two go back to the place where we left our ships," G-8 said. "I think you can take off if you do a little repair work. I'm going back into the castle to see if I can get in touch with *Herr Doktor* Frielinger."

Nippy slowed for a hairpin turn.

"So long," G-8 called. Then he dropped off into the road and started climbing directly up the side of the cliffs. It was a difficult job but he made it, arriving on top of the plateau once more, panting for breath. Far off, he could hear the angry, bellowing voice of *Stahlmaske*. Probably he was bawling out his men for permitting the prisoners to escape. The Master Spy crept nearer until he could make out the fiend's words:

"They think they can escape," he said, "but it is impossible. I will give them fifteen minutes to reach their planes. If they succeed by that time in repairing the damage that the wireless beam has done to their electrical apparatus, they will get another shot of the wireless beam. Some of you *dummkopfs* get these two cars working and go after them."

G-8 realized immediately that he had another job cut out for him. He must prevent *Stahlmaske* from turning on the deadly ray when Nippy and Bull were ready to take off. There was only one way to do that. He had located the electric wires that came into the castle by the light of the car as it sped down the hill. He remembered now where they entered the building. He must sever those connections just before *Herr Stahlmaske* was ready to turn on the beam. Otherwise, he might have time to find the break and repair it.

In the seclusion of a hollow between two rocks, G-8 took out his make-up kit and began remaking his face by the light that was part of the kit. For almost ten minutes he worked, manufacturing the most grotesque countenance possible with the few materials he had with him. He spread his nose out horribly, made his mouth appear twice as large and twisted. He built lumps on his cheek bones to make them stand out, then made his eyebrows larger and heavier. He had to admit that it wasn't nearly as ghastly as it might be, but he hoped it would do.

With the kit strapped once more in its place under his arm, he advanced to the point where the electric lines ran from a tree to a point on the side of a castle some ten feet from the ground. If he broke one wire, it would do the trick. He measured his distance in the light that slanted from the cracks in the walls and saw that there was a large limb extending above the wires. He climbed the tree, balanced on the limb and jumped feet first for the wires ten feet below. He caught a wire beneath the insteps of both feet and it sagged with his weight. Then there was a whistling snap as it severed and blue flame leaped up directly beneath him as the live wire contacted the ground.

G-8 fell in a heap dangerously near it, and leaped away instantly as the wire coiled and sprang back. The castle was instantly plunged into darkness. The Master Spy ran around the rear of the great structure and kept going until he reached the front.

Stahlmaske was shouting to his brutes to repair the line immediately. In the light of the blue flame that shot up from the live wire, G-8 saw one of the brutes seized by the shock and hurled a few feet away.

Under cover of that confusion, G-8 mingled with the ugly Huns, forced his way inside the castle and searched for the stairs that would lead to the only tower left. He was feeling his way up the ancient, spiralled steps when suddenly a voice barked out:

"Was ist?"

"Someone has cut the electric line," G-8 explained hastily. *"Herr Stahlmaske* sent me to get *Herr Doktor* Frielinger. He wants him brought down at once."

Keys jangled. It was so dark that G-8 could only sense the size of the guard. He strained to see how tall he was and to locate his face and head. The guard seemed to be having trouble unlocking the door, which gave G-8 the chance he was waiting for.

"Perhaps if I held your gun," he suggested, "you could use both hands."

"Of course," the brute agreed. He poked the bayoneted gun at the Master Spy and G-8 felt him turn his back, facing the door once more. G-8 turned the rifle about and stepped behind the guard so that the heavy butt was pointed at the base of the man's skull. He heard the key turn in the lock. That was his signal. He brought the rifle up like a pile driver and the other's body went limp as a rag. G-8 dragged it away. Still holding the rifle, he threw open the tower prison door and stepped inside.

"*Herr Doktor* Frielinger!" he whispered.

For a moment there was only a faint, rustling sound.

"*Herr Doktor* Frielinger," G-8 repeated. "I am G-8. I have come to help you. We must move fast while the lights are out. And you must tell me one thing."

"Anything," *Herr Doktor* Frielinger said in a meek voice, "except the secret of my beam. I will die before I give that up."

"Good," G-8 said. "But that isn't what I want to know."

He was already lifting the doctor, preparing to take him out.

"I want to know," the Master Spy said, "if there is any counter-acting beam that will neutralize the action of this disintegrating ray of yours."

"It is possible," Frielinger said. "If I had had a little more time in my laboratory to work it out, I could invent one. I had my plans for it all made. But you are an American spy, an enemy to the *Vaterland*."

"Yes," G-8 said. He threw the doctor over his shoulder as gently as he could and started for the door, carrying him fireman fashion.

"If you can get me and my wife and boy to France, I will do all in my power to develop the neutralizing beam that will combat the ray," the doctor promised. "If I die, the secret of the disintegrating beam dies with me. There is only one machine, *Herr Stahlmaske* has that."

"O. K.," G-8 said briefly. "Hang on. We're going to make a break for it."

He was almost running down the pitch-black stairs. He reached the banquet hall and realized, from the reflection of a blue light outside, that the wires had not yet been repaired.

The Master Spy could make out some figures near the door, but he must take a chance. The corridor into the moat was blocked off. He felt the stone paving of the hall underfoot and moved along the wall, working his way toward the door.

As he came nearer, he saw a crack in the great wall, some ten feet away from the door, that might serve as an exit. He tried to push through it. It was a tight squeeze, but he was making it. He reached the outside and tensed for a moment. The blue light had flared again, silhouetting him against the side of the building.

At the same instant, *Stahlmaske,* who had turned to stare inside, saw the Master Spy. He let out a wild roar of anger and drew his Luger. G-8 knew there was nothing to be gained by staying here, and that a wild break might save him, so he tried it. He plunged headlong into the thicket outside the castle. The Luger cracked. Other guns began barking. G-8 raced on and broke into a small clearing. The gun fire grew heavier. A bullet tore through his coat and creased his flesh.

Herr Doktor Frielinger, still lying across his shoulder like a bag of meal, gave a convulsive movement and emitted a gasp. Then his body went limp.

CHAPTER THIRTEEN
Death Rides the Dawn

Instantly, G-8 knew that the doctor had been hit. As he continued his mad charge across the open space, he dropped the rifle. A single clip of bullets wouldn't be much good to him. He pulled the doctor down from his shoulder and held him in his arms. He saw them that a bullet had blasted the skull of the doctor half apart. It was the end of *Herr Doktor* Frielinger. There was no use carrying him any farther.

But there was something on this person that G-8 must have. Awkwardly, the Master Spy searched for the tiny wireless set that must be somewhere about him. But *Stahlmaske* and his brutes were closing in. G-8 had enough of a lead so that he was sure of fifteen or twenty seconds before he would get be caught. He knew that the place was surrounded, for *Stahlmaske* had yelled, when he had dove into the thicket, "You cannot escape. All places of exit are guarded."

It was easy to understand how *Stahlmaske* had known that G-8 or someone opposed to him was still there. The break in the light line would tell him that.

G-8 found the little wireless set strapped to the inside of *Herr Doktor* Frielinger's left leg where it wouldn't be easily noticed. Running and carrying the body as he was now, G-8 had difficulty in detaching it. He dropped the doctor suddenly in a clump of brush, knelt down, and quickly loosened the thin box, slipping it into his boot top. He then ran on, but his escape was short-lived.

In the early morning light, grotesque figures rose at the edge of the cliffs and held guns pointed at G-8's middle. The Master Spy stopped. A few seconds later, *Stahlmaske* and the others caught up with him. While two brutes held the Master Spy, *Stahlmaske* struck him across the face with the palm of his hand. It was a brutal blow that nearly floored G-8.

"You tricked me once," *Stahlmaske* rasped. "But you shall not do it again."

He turned to his brutes and ordered, "Take him into the dungeon once more and hold him there until we have the electric line repaired and the balloon is ready to go up. Then I shall use him for my test."

Once more G-8 was thrown into the dungeon, this time alone. There was almost no hope of getting out alive, but if he could contact Nippy or Bull, there would be a good chance of destroying *Stahlmaske*, his brutes, and the death beam.

The door closed behind him. Daylight was filtering through the slits in the dungeon as G-8 took *Herr Doktor* Frielinger's little wireless set from his boot. He turned the switch over to the sending terminal and began ticking off his message:

NIPPY AND BULL. NIPPY AND BULL. IF YOU CAN HEAR ME ANSWER.

He switched back to the receiving post and listened. No answer came. In five minutes he repeated that call and again each five minutes for half an hour. Then a reply came.

O. K. WE MADE NANCY. REFUELING. WHAT'S UP?

Frantically, G-8 began ticking out orders:

BRING ALL PLANES FROM NAN-
CY AS QUICKLY AS POSSIBLE.
COME TO LA ROCQUE CASTLE. FLY
MAXIMUM CEILING. BOMB EN-
TIRE CASTLE AND CLIFFS. EVERY-
THING MUST BE DESTROYED.

The answer came back:

BUT WHERE WILL YOU BE?

G-8 hastened to assure his Battle Aces.

I'M GETTING AWAY. DON'T WOR-
RY ABOUT ME. BLOW EVERY-
THING TO BITS.

Then he heard:

O. K. WE'RE COMING.

G-8 whirled in sudden alarm at a sound
outside the dungeon door. He turned just
in time to see flame spurt from the muzzle
of a Luger that was poked through the
grill. The tiny wireless machine that he
had held on his knee flew apart, and in
the next instant, *Herr Stahlmaske's* fiendish laugh rang through the dungeon.

"Das ist gut," he chuckled. "You have

been calling your assistants. *Und* I know what you have told them. You have given them orders to bring over planes *und* blow up La Rocque Castle." He laughed again. "*Ja, das ist gut.* We shall be ready you and I. I was going to kill you first, but now you shall see what happens to *them* before you die. You will have—what do you call it in America?—a ringside seat."

He turned to his brutes and commanded, "Bring him out."

Minutes sped by while G-8 was taken from the dungeon and transported by car to the very field where he had shot down *Herr Stahlmaske.* Under the trees at the side of the field he saw a large captive balloon straining at the winch. There was much activity going on.

Herr Stahlmaske brought the Master Spy an American uniform.

"Put this on," he commanded. "Your assistants and the other *verdammt* Allies shall know that you are an American. They will not dare destroy me or the balloon for fear of injurying you. In the meantime, I shall destroy them"—he made a puffing sound with his mouth—"like that."

G-8 said nothing. He was powerless to do anything to free himself. The brutes were tying him to one side of the basket with stout ropes bound around his arms, legs, and waist.

More minutes passed while preparations for the ascent were completed, then *Stahlmaske* climbed into the balloon basket. He leered through his mask at the Master Spy and pointed the strange-looking weapon at him. G-8 saw the long electric cables running from the winch over to the machines of coils and tubes.

"All I have to do is pull this trigger," *Stahlmaske* chuckled, "and where you stand now there will be nothing but a vacant hole. You and the side of the basket and the ropes will vanish."

From far to the southwest, G-8 heard a rumbling sound. *Stahlmaske* heard it, too, and turned quickly to give orders to his brute men.

"Rise the balloon," he rasped. "They are coming."

The winch growled as it released the giant bag. G-8 and *Stahlmaske* shot into the air and rose rapidly.

The Master Spy could see a great swarm of planes storming out of the southwest over the northern tip of the Vosges mountains. He couldn't pick Nippy and Bull out of the mass, but he knew they were there.

Above the roar of the engines, *Stahl-*

maske laughed triumphantly. With all his might, G-8 strained at the ropes that bound him. He must get free and stop this wholesale murder that was going to take place! Suddenly, something snapped behind him. He guessed that it was one of the reeds in the basket that pulled loose, but whatever it was, it gave him more freedom of motion. The ropes grew slack. He was slipping out of them.

Stahlmaske braced himself against the corner of the basket and raised the death machine to aim it at the lead plane, an S.E. 5 loaded with bombs. Behind it, on either side, flew Nippy and Bull.

Stahlmaske screamed with fiendish glee and pulled the trigger. G-8 was staring open-mouthed as he struggled to get the last of the ropes off. Part of the S.E. 5 was vanishing. The whole center, including the fusilage, engine, and the inner half of the wings, suddenly disappeared. For a brief instant, there was a slight trace of the members that had made up the gaping hole. The wingstips and outer struts, which were the only things remaining of the plane, began falling by themselves.

With another scream of triumph, *Herr Stahlmaske* turned his way toward Spad number 13. But G-8 was throwing off the last rope. He leaped for the beast, grabbed his shoulder and hurled him back off his balance. With his right hand, he reached over and grasped the wireless instrument, jerking it partly out of the steel-masked fiend's hand.

With a roar, *Stahlmaske* turned on him, still clutching the machine in his left hand. He had enormous strength—twice that of the Master Spy! G-8 would be little more than a rag doll in his hands if he didn't act quickly.

Stahlmaske's left arm that still clutched the machine was against the edge of the basket. With a lightning movement, G-8 brought his right fist down on the arm. The blow fell on a vital nerve center. If it was hard enough, it would numb the entire arm. G-8 saw the beam gun drop over the side of the basket and knew that he had won that point!

What happened after that was rather hazy in the Master Spy's mind. He and *Stahlmaske* were fighting furiously in that small balloon basket. The steel-mask protected *Stahlmaske's* head from any possible injury, so G-8 concentrated on his middle. Suddenly, the air went out of the Master Spy. Then he sensed vaguely that he was going

189

over the side, grabbing a parachute harness as he dove.

Machine guns were shattering the air and bombs were exploding below him. A crack just above told him that his parachute had opened. He hung on desperately to the harness that he hadn't had time to put on.

Even with his senses dulled, these moments were a nightmare to the Master Spy. Death, the grim pursuer who seemed to haunt his every day, was leering still in mockery at his side. Then his head cleared a bit as the frightful vision passed out of his jumbled thoughts.

A great ball of flame—all that was left of the captive balloon—was settling down on him. He saw *Stahlmaske* leaning over the edge of the basket. Brutes were running from the field and the Allied planes were after them, bombing and straffing them as they went.

Suddenly, the Master Spy knew he was down. His head struck something hard and things became more hazy about him than ever. Next, he was being picked up and carried off. There was the vibration of a motor.

Regaining consciousness, he knew he was

tied to the wing of a Spad. He stared up into the grinning face of Nippy Weston.

"Good morning," the terrier ace shouted. "And how would you like your eggs this morning?"

G-8 grinned back.

"Sunny side up," he answered.

And that's the way they were, for Battle had breakfast ready shortly after their return.

It was good to look about and see his pals and faithful Battle, G-8 thought. These moments of reunion, with death and disaster finally overcome, seemed to be worth the effort. It did not, however, compensate for the thousands of lives eaten away each day by the ravaging hands of War. It did not, for example, bring back to life these airmen who had died to satisfy the bloodlust of *Stahlmaske*. But now, for a time at least, G-8's mind turned to happier thoughts and events.

"Boy!" Bull exploded as he sat down to the table. "It sure is a pleasure to get back to one of Battle's good meals."

"The main thing I'm looking forward to," G-8 said, "is taking a shower and dressing in—"

"Oh, I say," Battle cut in eagerly. "Beggin' your pardon, sir, but that's it. I've got it!"

Three faces turned to stare blankly at the English manservant.

"Got what?" Bull demanded.

"Why, the rest of that joke, sir," Battle explained.

"You mean," demanded Nippy, "that you just thought of the answer to that joke you started more than a month ago?"

"Oh, quite," Battle enthused. "Yes, I've got it. Now don't stop me. I must say it before I forget it. The answer is because it sees the salad dressing."

"What's all this about?" G-8 asked, "This salad dressing business?"

"It's about the joke, sir," Battle said. "You remember! I tried to work it over a month ago and I couldn't think of the end? All I could think of was 'because it saw the mayonnaise,' and that wasn't right. And now I have it. 'Because it sees the salad dressing!' That's the same thing as mayonnaise, isn't it?"

"Sure," G-8 laughed. "Let's try it again, Battle, and see if we can get the whole thing straight. Go on, you ask me."

Battle's face grew suddenly blank.

"Oh, I say," he groaned in dismay. "Dash it all, now I've forgotten the first part of it!"